Holly Hill Mangin

The House on the Lake

To infinity and beyond.

And to those I love that much.

The House on the Lake

by Holly Hill Mangin

# Chapter 1

**T**he first thing I'm aware of is the light filtering through my eyelids. It's not the bright, perky light that alerts one straightaway that it's morning, nor is it the artificial fluorescence belonging to flickering overhead lamps. It's muted. Gray. Just there, a constant, irritating presence.

Rolling over, I commit myself to falling back to sleep, but the gray pallor invades and prompts the nagging feeling that I'm not where I usually am when I wake up. The smell is different, slightly musty, like the windows have been left open during a storm, and from the extra firm feel of the mattress, this isn't my bed. And the light . . . it *should* be shining in from the right side of the bed but is coming from the left.

*What the hell?*

My eyes pop open and seconds later, I'm fully awake and rigidly sitting in a strange bed in a strange room. My eyes dart from one thing to the next, trying to find something familiar, something to ground me, but there's nothing. I open my mouth to call out only to smother my cry at the last moment, wondering if it will bring some unwanted stranger with unwanted ideas. Panic looms in my chest, a weight that threatens to pull me down even as I struggle with the sheets entangling my limbs, tying me to the bed from which I'm trying to free myself. Whimpering, I pull at the twisted bedding, my fear hampering my progress. Breathing hard, I yank once more and almost fall to the floor.

I pass my hands over my eyes and slap my cheeks a few times to jog my memory. It doesn't help. And worse, the disturbing suspicion that someone is watching my every move overwhelms me. I look around, my hands clutching the bottom edge of my oversized T-shirt and pulling it down to my thighs. Two doors stand partially open, and I quickly glance into each room—a bathroom and closet—before pulling them both shut. The dark void beneath the bed mocks me, so I drop to my knees to inspect under there as well.

I'm alone.

I take a few deep breaths and try to calm my racing heart. There's no immediate danger, but I'm not about to let down my guard. I lick my lips, swallow, and rise to my feet, frowning. Glancing furtively around me, I slink to a window to get my bearings. I want to know what I'm up against. I see trees; I see I'm on the second story of a house, a pretty large one from what I can tell; I see that there are no people around, and I see water. Lots of it.

I'm deathly afraid of water.

Opening the window and lifting the screen, I lean out over the ledge—heights don't bother me. But as I inspect my surroundings, all I can discern are the undulating ripples of an endless expanse of water. There's a yard, sure, but my eyes aren't drawn to the mundane. All my mind can grasp are the waves gently lapping the shore. Gently lapping. My fingernails dig into the ledge. *Who am I kidding?* They're crashing, pounding, banging as far as I'm concerned.

My stomach turns, and I shove away from the window. Usually, I have no problem looking at water. When I sit on a beach, I can watch the waves for hours, their hypnotizing movement lulling me into a sense of calm, but unless I'm taking a shower or drinking a glass of it, I won't go near it. I *can*. But it's not advised. Swimming? Forget it. And now, being in a place I don't recognize with a whole bunch of it literally dozens of yards before me? Not helping anything.

I force myself to breathe in and out slowly and close my eyes to focus solely on inhaling and exhaling. I learned this technique in meditation classes, and it has always helped in the past, but instead of soothing me, I imagine streams of bluish-green water invading my nostrils and filling my mouth.

Gasping, I drop to my knees and crawl over to the bed. I yank the blanket off to wrap around me, over me, hiding me away, protecting me from the liquid that threatens to swallow me alive. I'd almost prefer there be a stranger in the room to the knowledge of what's out there surrounding the house. Once again, I focus on my breathing. Inhale, exhale, breathe, relax, and for the next few minutes, these four words become my mantra as my mind whirls with my terror, and I fight to hold on to all I *do* know.

My name is Eve. I'm twenty-eight. I know where I work. I know where I live. I know what I had for breakfast yesterday morning down to the number of bacon slices. Today should be Sunday. I never sleep past seven, and although there's no clock, I'm banking on that still being the case. What else? Oh yeah, there's a hell of a lot of water out there, and I'm sitting under a blanket on the floor of a strange room, talking to myself about what I remember so I don't drive myself crazy thinking about the things I forgot.

Wait. *Relax, Reflect, Release.*

The words pop into my head at the same time as the certainty that I'm on a retreat. The memory is vague, negligible, but it's enough for me to cling to, and cling I do. I let the blanket drop below my shoulders and open my eyes. The room, though dark with the drab light coming in through

4

the window, is quite big. There's a seating area in one corner with two overstuffed chairs and accompanying poufs and a square table between the chairs large enough to accommodate a breakfast tray in addition to the small lamp that already sits there. The bed is one of those four-poster deals with voluminous white sheets pushed to each of the four corners. The floors are made of white oak, and everything from the chairs to the bed to the oversized rug is decorated in shades of white, creams, and beiges. Of course, I'm on a retreat.

My eyes widen as I remember. I found this place in an ad—an old Victorian manor in a remote location renting out rooms for solo retreats. There were no pictures, and the luxury of the room is not what I was expecting. The ad made the place sound old, antiquated, even a bit rundown. I vaguely remember something about a haunting as well, and it's exactly the reason I wanted to come. My sister and I absolutely love the strange and bizarre, and she's totally into any place that could potentially contain anything paranormal. I thought I'd check the place out on my own—I was due a week of vacation anyway—and getting away from the hustle and bustle of everyday life had me thinking the place being a retreat would just be a bonus. If it turned out to be nothing more than an old house, I wouldn't have wasted my sister's time.

I walk over to the door of the bathroom and peek inside. Now that I'm actually focusing, it's just as luxurious as the room in which I obviously slept. I smile. Not too shabby. Then, I walk over to the closet, open it, and look in at where all my clothes are already hanging and placed on shelves.

But I don't remember doing that.

Suddenly the calm I felt in remembering where I am turns to anxiety over all the things I'm forgetting, like how I got here, where here is exactly, and why I'm having such a hard time remembering everything in the first place. There's something else I'm forgetting too. I know there is. A memory niggles at the back of my mind like the words of a song that are just on the tip of my tongue. The thought eludes me, delving deeper into the folds of my mind to escape my grasp.

Grabbing a pair of capris and a yellow tunic, I quickly go through my morning routine. I can sit here and wait for the answers to come to me, or I can go out and find them, and although I hate having to ask for help, more from timidity than actually receiving it, I know that in this case, it has to be done.

Inhaling deeply, I look to the last door in the room, the one that's firmly shut, and tossing one last glance at the room around me, I throw my shoulders back and march toward it.

It's time to get some answers.

Chapter 2

◆•————————•————————•◆

**I** don't know which way to turn when I step out of the doorway. A long, dimly lit hall of equal distance on either side of the door meets my gaze. The hall is nothing like the bedroom I just left. Dark wood wainscoting covers the walls from floor to ceiling, and the dim light is coming from electric sconces spaced roughly six feet apart. The floors are also of dark wood, maybe walnut, giving me the feeling that I'm entering a tunnel or a funhouse. Choosing to go right, I quietly make my way, trying to be as quiet as possible in case other residents are resting or sleeping. I pass by door upon door, at least a dozen, many of them open. I try to look into them peripherally, but I don't see much, and I don't dare to peer into the rooms straight-on lest I see someone glaring at me for having the audacity to do so.

There's no noise besides my footsteps, and I start to wonder if I went the wrong direction when I see the same dull gray light from my bedroom streaming in through a stained-glass window at the end of the hall. The colors cascade from their Art Deco design onto the walnut floor just in front of it. The soft, muted, soothing peaches and greens all but disappear, almost as if they are absorbed, when they reach the flooring. The window is on a landing with a staircase that splits off in opposite directions, the front and back of the house, I assume. One set of stairs is wider and grander than the other, and I choose those to walk down. I don't want to go to parts of the house that are off limits, and the "good" stairs are for guests, or so I've read.

So far, despite the water outside, the inside's in keeping with what I was hoping for. It's eclectic and a bit creepy and definitely has potential as a place I would bring my sister. I hope there are scary stories about it, mysterious and strange. And it would be really cool if there was a ghost or two—as long as they were more like Casper and less like the green blob in *Ghostbusters*.

Walking down the stairs, I can picture it at Christmas with garland and fairy lights woven between the railings, and when I get to the bottom, opposite the stairs is a living room, again in sharp contrast to the hallway and stairs I just left. It has vaulted ceilings and overstuffed couches and chairs. In keeping with similar décor from the bedroom, everything is elegant and stylish—in hues of cream, beige and brown—yet understated and calming.

I pass by several closed doors and come upon the kitchen. It's not empty. From the doorway, I watch as an older man and woman prepare breakfast, and the way they move tells me they've been with one another for a long time. They move through the kitchen in synchronization, their own little dance. The man opens an upper cupboard just as the woman bends over to put something in the dishwasher. When she rises, he arches his arm and turns sideways to allow her to pass by him without touching. By the time he takes out two coffee mugs and places them on the counter, she has gracefully turned around to drop in two tea bags and pour boiling water from the kettle she took from the stove. They smile at each other, and I'm tempted to back out of the room to allow them their privacy. The woman sees me though, and their moment is gone.

"Well now! Look what we have here. Good morning!" the woman exclaims as I walk into the room. The man gives a wave of his hand. Shyly, I make my way around the kitchen, my back straight but my eyes lowered. "Good morning," I mumble, feeling awkward. "I smelled breakfast. Smells good."

"Why, thank you! And there's plenty of it. Sit yourself down at the table and let me fix you up a plate." The woman smiles as she leads me to a chair. It's a kind smile, and then she pointedly regards the man before going over and opening a cupboard to get a plate.

The man clears his throat, nods at me in acknowledgment, and begins to speak. "The name's Hammond. This here—" he points to the woman— "is Gail." He clears his throat again. "I guess you'd call us the caretakers of the manor."

Their familiarity with the place makes sense. "It's nice to meet you. I'm Eve."

Gail smiles. "We know."

A frown furrows my brow. "This is going to sound crazy, but I—" I look around the kitchen, wondering how I'm going to sound when I tell them. "I really have no idea *where* this place is or how I got here."

Gail again eyes Hammond and then comes over to sit in the chair beside me, an empty plate in her hand. "What do you remember, dear?"

"I know that this is a manor offering individual rooms for solo retreats, but that's pretty much it. I don't remember anything else. I mean, I must have gotten here yesterday considering I woke up in a bedroom upstairs—very comfortable, by the way—but that's about it. Is anyone else here?"

"We like to keep to ourselves," Hammond practically spits. It doesn't sound like he carries the same opinion as the *we* he refers to.

Gail tsks at Hammond before turning back to me. "This house used to thrive," she says with a smile. "But for the last decade or so, we've taken a hit. Perhaps it's something we've done . . ." For a moment, she's quiet before she shakes her head as if to dispel unpleasant thoughts, then smiles again and gets up to walk to the stove. "But you're here now," she says while she loads up the plate, "and maybe that's exactly what is needed."

Gail brings back the plate heaped with bacon, eggs, and toast, sets it in front of me, and takes a seat beside me once again. Hammond goes to the refrigerator, takes out some orange juice, and grabs a glass from the cupboard before bringing both over to the table. He then collects the mugs of tea and sets one in front of Gail before sitting across from me with the other.

"So, where are we exactly? Why don't I remember anything?"

"I suppose you'll remember when you're good and ready," says Hammond gruffly. "People are always in a hurry to get things all squared away. Give yourself a chance."

I take a bite of the eggs and nod. He has a point. My mom always says that patience is a virtue—not one I was born with very much of. And it did take me a little while to remember why I'm here.

"I think when you got here, you had a bit of a shock," Gail says, her eyes filled with meaning.

*The water. Of course.* "Did I faint or something? I saw the water from the bedroom window… I-I'm afraid of water."

"You know, that may be it. We are on an island, you know."

"Wait, we're on an island?"

"Why, yes."

"That's impossible." I shake my head as if that will change anything. There is no way I would step foot on a boat unless the boat was on land and planning on staying there, so how I made it onto an island, I have no idea.

"Can you tell me anything else? Is there anyone else here?" I asked before and wasn't given a straight answer. I wonder if I'll get one this time.

Gail opens her mouth once again to speak, but Hammond only glances at her with his dark eyes and she closes it as if afraid she might say something that would go against his wishes. He turns to me and I feel uncomfortable under his scrutiny. He's tall and formidable and reminds me in both looks and mannerisms of Lurch, the manservant from *The Addams Family*. At length, he opens his mouth and even though I've already heard him speak, I expect one of Lurch's inarticulate moans and am surprised by actual words. "We don't get many visitors anymore. You're the first one."

My eyes widen in shock. "In a decade?"

Hammond harrumphs and Gail nods. I should feel troubled about the circumstances of my arrival, and I do. There's no reason I should forget how I got here, but the house is getting more and more interesting, and the circumstances of my arrival are seeming less and less important.

Gail misinterprets my silence as uneasiness. "Oh, you poor dear. I'm sure it'll all come back to you eventually. You just need to relax and reflect."

Relax and reflect. It's what I remembered earlier, and it makes me wonder if I've met Gail before, even though she's not familiar. "You said you knew who I was. Did I meet you yesterday?"

"We couldn't meet you yesterday." I'm kind of surprised Hammond speaks up again, and when my eyes move across to him, he isn't looking at me but at Gail. "We were busy."

It's so abrupt; I'm waiting for there to be more, but there's nothing but silence.

13

"I'm sorry, Eve. Is your breakfast cold? Do you want me to heat it up for you?"

Both Gail and Hammond get up from the table, and Gail snatches my plate before I have a chance to tell her not to worry. Within seconds, she places a fresh plate of food in front of me and Hammond is gathering the mugs of tea, although I don't think I saw either of them so much as take a sip.

Whereas Hammond favors Frankenstein's monster, complete with a somewhat disheveled black jacket, Gail looks like someone's friendly grandmother. Her hair is pulled up in a stereotypical bun, the wrinkles around her eyes make me think she's only shown kindness, and she's wearing a long-sleeved gray dress that whispers against her ankles and is covered by a long white apron. I can only hope her demeanor matches her appearance, which so far seems encouraging, even though I haven't been in the presence of either long enough to know much at all.

I take a few bites of the eggs and then eat a piece of bacon. The details of the retreat may be foggy, but what's foremost in my mind is whether I'll be able to explore or if I'll be relegated to only a few rooms. My heart is hammering in my chest, but I have to ask. "Do you mind if I look through the rooms? I'm not just restricted to my room and here, am I?"

Hammond snorts, and when I glance at him, I see a genuine smile. "No, child. You're not our hostage, you know. You came to us, remember?" He chuckles and then loses his smile as he gives a wet cough before continuing. "You'll have access to all the rooms for your explorations." He nods his head to emphasize his declaration. "No sense being here without looking into things. Just realize that there may be some rooms you won't be able to go into on certain days. Our work requires us to close some rooms off occasionally."

I nod my head enthusiastically, unable to tamp down on my excitement of being able to explore the whole manor. "I totally understand. I don't want to intrude. If I'm somewhere I'm not supposed to be, just tell me."

Gail smiles and comes over to pat my shoulder. "This is your home while you're here, so there's no reason not to see as much as you can. Everyone should be comfortable in their home. Don't you agree?"

Before I can nod, she tilts her head and her eyes become distant. "Everybody needs to take account of their lives at some point. Looking at the past helps us figure out the future and all that." She shakes her head and her eyes once again focus on me. "You make sure to come see us if you're ever feeling lonely though."

Gail pats my back again, and although I'm not in the habit of having people I just met touch me, the warm press of her hand is reassuring. "You're here now. Enjoy the time you're with us, won't you?"

Before I can answer, Gail inhales sharply, her spine rigid as she stares toward the door I entered. Her eyes hold disbelief, and I'm almost frightened to turn around. I do though, and gape at the person I see every day in the mirror and the one I grew up sharing secrets with. Lyn stares back with wide eyes and an O-shaped mouth.

"Eve," she exclaims, rushing forward.

I feel a mixture of relief and dread at seeing her. Relief because I won't be doing this alone. It's always more fun to have someone else tagging along, especially when there's the possibility of finding something strange and unusual. And dread because, because, and that's where I stop. I don't know why I feel dread or if it's dread at all. Maybe it's just disappointment. Not at Lyn, but maybe because she's here? It's all so contradictory—my feelings and my logic as well.

Hoping my emotions don't show on my face, I spring out of my chair and hug Lyn. I may be feeling some misgivings, but she's a reminder of the life I have away from all this, and I love her.

"What are you doing here?" I ask, pulling away from her so I can see her face.

"What am *I* doing here? Eve, what are *we* doing here?" Lyn demands at the same time Gail's voice has become a stunned squawk as she moves around the room for no apparent reason, her arms flapping in the air.

"This is highly irregular! Highly irregular, indeed!"

And Hammond is muttering, "Well, this is interesting," as he eyes my sister with curiosity.

For a few moments, all is chaos.

➤ The House on the Lake

## Chapter 3

Lyn is yelling, Gail is pacing—I swear she's going to tear her fingers off, she's wringing them so much—and Hammond is looking down at the floor, shaking his head and muttering to himself. We just need a dog barking and an alarm going off, and the scene would be a perfect cliché.

There's no dog and no alarm, but that doesn't mean I'm not getting a headache. "Can you guys be quiet?" I ask in what I hope is a calm, rational voice. Lyn glances over at me but continues her tirade, screaming about how she knows people and will bring down the wrath of God if we're not returned, unharmed, back to our houses immediately.

That's Lyn. She acts first and asks questions later. She always has. In some ways, it's intimidating as hell, especially when you're on the receiving end of one of her blasts, but man, it has to be freeing too. I envy her freedom. Even when younger, I could nail down Lyn's personality in my head and rant with the best of them, telling off everyone I thought had done me wrong, but when I opened my mouth, well, the words never sounded the same—if they came out at all. It was the one aspect of her personality I could never get down out loud.

But I'm feeling brave today.

I look Lyn directly in the eye. "Shut. Up. Now! Stop talking."

She opens her mouth to say something more and I hiss, straightening my back and giving her my most withering glare.

Yeah, it *is* freeing.

"Let's figure all of this out like rational adults, shall we?" I throw another glare at my sister before turning back to Gail and Hammond. Gail is still wringing her hands, but she has thankfully stopped pacing. All Hammond needs is a disembodied hand sitting on his shoulder, and he wouldn't just remind me of Lurch, he would be the spitting image.

I sit at the table, suddenly overwhelmingly tired. Rubbing my eyes, I look at Lyn. "This is my retreat." I know it, but it still sounds so bizarre, even to me, and I have to repeat myself. "I'm here on a retreat. What are you doing here?"

Lyn looks at me as if I've suddenly sprouted horns and taken up eating worms. I really can't blame her. "You're here on a retreat? Really? Then what am I doing here?"

"That's what I just asked you when you came in." I tap the table and Lyn comes over and sits next to me.

"I don't remember!" With elbows on the table, she covers her eyes with her hands. All is silent for a few seconds as she thinks, and while she's thinking, so am I.

I'm thinking that it's really weird I'm so detached from all of this. In some corner of my mind, I care that this is happening, but it's like I'm numb to it all, watching everything through the lens of a camera as it happens to someone else. I'm thinking that there's no way anyone would get me on an island without drugging me or knocking me out, and while I don't feel the greatest, I don't think it's drug-induced or that Hammond, formidable as he appears, is capable of knocking me over the head, let alone knocking out my sister. I'm beginning to think I'm dreaming because yeah, that would pretty much be the only thing that makes sense.

From behind her hands, Lyn finally mutters, "Eve, what the hell? This is messed up." She scans the room, her eyes landing on Gail and Hammond.

Yes, my parents raised me better, *us* better, but with all the drama . . . "I'm sorry—Gail, Hammond—this is Lyn. Lyn, Gail and Hammond are the caretakers for the house."

Lyn stands up and walks over to them. Gail shrinks away when Lyn thrusts out her hand, but when she sees my sister's hand is empty, she extends her own trembling fingers and shakes. Despite the appearance of docility, her grip, I'm for some reason secretly pleased to see, is just as firm as Lyn's. Lyn turns to Hammond next, taking his hand as well. "It's nice to meet you both. I'm sorry for my outburst earlier, but waking up in a strange place with no knowledge of how I got there tends to put me a bit on edge." Lyn points over to me. "Perhaps you already explained to Eve, but can you tell me what's going on?"

As Gail did with me earlier, she leads Lyn back to the table and sits her down before going over and getting a plate, which she begins to load. "Uh, ah, we were only expecting one of you." She continues to pile on the eggs and when she notices the amount, she tilts the plate, emptying it to start again. "You showing up . . ." Her head swivels to Lyn as if to make sure she's still there. "I don't . . . I can't . . ."

Hammond takes the plate from Gail and brings it over to Lyn. He then returns to Gail and leads her over to the table to sit.

Lyn and I look at each other and I reach out a hand toward Gail. "You said you were busy when I got here yesterday, which is why you didn't meet me. It's obvious you didn't know Lyn was here. Is there someone else we can talk to?"

"In a sense."

I'm getting pretty tired of all the talking without saying anything. "What does that mean?"

Gail sighs in exasperation, and for a brief moment, her eyes darken with anger and her mouth takes on a scowl. "I don't—"

Hammond clears his throat and pointedly frowns at Gail, at her raised voice and harsh tone.

She schools her face and takes a deep breath. "Girls, I don't know what to tell you. I just try to keep things running around here. Hammond and I both do. You'll have to talk to—talk to the owner to find out what's going on."

"Who is the owner? Where is he or she?" asks Lyn.

Gail wrings her hands again and turns to Hammond as if the answer is written on his high forehead. "Uh, around. Perhaps you can ask Nick."

Hammond stands, and I feel like I have to crane my neck to look up at him as he takes in both Lyn and me. "Gail, we have somewhere we need to be. Eve—" he bows slightly— "Lyn," he nods. "We'll be around."

Gail rises from her chair. "Yes, we must be going. Remember, you're here to relax, reflect, release. Okay? No worries while you're here." Once more she pats my shoulder. "If you need anything, let us know."

23

They walk away, their heads close together, and turn to regard us once more when they get to the door. The last thing I hear is Gail's, "highly irregular," as they pass through the door and go someplace I have yet to explore.

As soon as their footsteps fade down the hall, Lyn wrings her hands. "If you need anything, let us know," she mimics. "How about some friggin' answers, huh?" She rolls her eyes and takes a bite of the eggs. "Who's Nick?"

"I have no idea."

"So, you have no idea where you are, but you know you're supposed to be here," she says, using air quotes and rolling her eyes. "You sound brainwashed." She sticks a few more forkfuls of eggs into her mouth. "Mmm, this is good. Did you tell Mom and Dad you were coming here?"

Normally, Lyn is pretty polite, even if there's no one around besides me. The finger-licking, I-don't-give-a-fuck attitude emanating from her is all a front. She's scared, and I'm not. It's a role reversal I wish I could savor, but I'm not a monster.

"'Relax, reflect, release.' I woke up with that in my head," I say, ignoring her questions. "I really don't think we're in any danger, do you? I mean, seriously, if something was off, my intuition would be screaming right now. And you'd be freaking out way more than you are."

Lyn puts down her fork and sighs. "True. I mean, even though I hate not knowing what's going on—*hate* it—I don't feel threatened."

I giggle. "You scared Gail half to death, I think."

Lyn snorts. "And what crawled up Hammond's butt?"

The orange juice I was just taking a sip of sprays from my mouth. "Shhh, what if they're listening?

"Then maybe they'll finally tell us what the hell is going on," she says, raising her voice at the end. Lyn picks up her empty plate and mine and carries them over to the sink where she rinses them off and then sticks them in the dishwasher to the side. "I have to admit, though. This place screams your name."

"What do you mean?"

She turns around, resting her lower back against the counter. "It's just so you. I don't know. I woke up this morning, and my room was all fluffy and light colors. I know you like that stuff 'cuz you always point it out in catalogs, and I noticed your apartment is getting more and more Scandinavian Farmhouse, and I was like, Eve would love this. Pretty much everything I've laid my eyes on is something you'd be wild about for some reason or another."

I laugh. "Wow, I'm impressed. You've got the terminology down and everything."

"I do listen to you every now and then," Lyn smirks before she frowns a little. "What are we going to do?"

"Well, they seem docile enough. They fed us; we're in an awesome house from what I've seen so far."

"I suppose. Still . . . do you have your phone? I couldn't find mine."

"Seriously? I'm always forgetting my phone. Probably because no one calls me."

"Stop whining," she says. This is a conversation we've had before. She always tells me the phone can be used two ways, that I can call out, not just receive messages. Obviously, I know this, but I'm not like Lyn. I don't have a bunch of friends like she does. And no, I'm not complaining. I have a few close friends, and I like it that way. Sometimes I go out; most often I stay in. Nothing wrong with that.

"Anyway, is one supposed to bring a phone on a retreat?" I ask because I know it will rile her up. It does.

"We're *not* on a retreat! There's something messed up about all of this, and we're going to figure it out."

"Fine. Yes, we'll figure it out, but for right now, can we just relax? Breathe." I raise and lower my hands as if I'm trying to temper a beast.

Lyn swats my hands away and glances around the kitchen. "We might as well look for a phone somewhere. I don't think Grumpy and Scaredy would give us one if we asked for it."

I laugh again. I love her. Yes, I still say it would be nice just to relax and be by myself for a few days, but Lyn's got this personality you can't help but want to be around. It's like she's this light and people are drawn to her. A worn-out cliché, I know, but that's Lyn—a worn-out, but hard to deny cliché.

I take a sponge from the sink and wipe off the kitchen table, removing the remaining mugs and glasses as I do so. I may be a guest here, but I was raised to clean up after myself, and I was never one to be waited on.

When I'm satisfied, I nod at Lyn. "Where do you want to start first? Hammond said I have access to all the rooms. I'm sure that extends to you too. That doesn't really sound like someone who is keeping us here against our will, does it?"

Lyn narrows her eyes and gives a huff. "We'll see," she says, but then she brightens. "Maybe we can find this Nick person and ask him what's going on. Start up and work our way down?"

I smile. She wants to poke around as much as I do. "It's highly irregular," I start, and Lyn hits me playfully on the arm.

"But we might as well," I say. "It's always good to be thorough."

"My thoughts exactly."

## Chapter 4

**W**e are planning to start on the floor we both woke up on when, on the landing with the stained-glass window I admired earlier, I find a concealed narrow door slightly ajar.

"He said I could go anywhere I want." My jaw is set and even as I say the words, I know I'm not going to let Lyn talk me out of exploring.

"Yeah, but did he know you were going to find a secret passageway?"

"That makes it all the more fun."

"True. After you."

It's as if we enter a different world. Gone are the dark wainscoting and walnut flooring. Instead, a murky, narrow staircase leads up. I find a light switch and turn it on. The yellowed bulb of a hanging light flickers at first before casting a steady albeit dim light from its ball-chained shackle. It's little more than what we had before, but its added glow and the faint buzz of electricity that accompanies it are welcomed nonetheless.

The stairwell doesn't look as if it is about to come tumbling down, but it doesn't seem to have been touched in a very long time either. The whites and creams from the bedroom are gone, exchanged for dirt and grit on warped, timeworn floorboards, and shadows I suspect are mildew stains coat the walls and ceiling in places. Dust and cobwebs blanket the floors and weave themselves in high corners, and as we make our way to the top of the stairs, a room opens before us filled with discarded and broken furniture, boxes, and knickknacks haphazardly piled on tables and the floor. It's exactly what I believe I would see if I were to visit the attic of Miss Havisham from *Great Expectations*. I clap my hands together and practically beam at Lyn, whose lips are scrunched up in distaste.

"Nick? Oh, Nick?" Lyn calls out two steps from the top. She snaps her fingers. "Darn, he doesn't seem to be here. Come on, let's go."

"No! We have to look around a little. Come on, this is so cool. We could even organize it a little, and—"

"You are such a freak."

I bounce on my toes and clasp my hands while I give her puppy dog eyes.

"Oh, fine! If you're planning on spending all day up here though, I'm going back down to my room."

I nod in agreement, and my gaze touches upon everything as they wander across the room. Not only does it run the entire length of the house, but the ceiling is almost twice the height, reminiscent of the ceiling in the living room I saw earlier. My focus is drawn to the wall of floor-to-ceiling windows, moth-eaten velvety curtains drawn, along one length of the large expanse, and with my eyes pulled more or less upwards, I slowly walk in until I stand at the center, in front of a massive fireplace made of what looks like white and black marble. Why all of this would be wasted in an attic is beyond me, and amazed, I simply gawk.

Spinning in a slow circle, I take it all in. "Can you believe this?" I ask Lyn, finding her examining some portraits of what must be dour-looking men and women gazing out unseeingly into the room from the wall opposite the windows and on the same wall as the fireplace. The dim light hides their expressions from me at this distance, but I can feel the weight of their stares as the colorful, large and medium-sized frames in which they rest compete for the attention of the room's occupants.

"It's wild," she agrees, her face filled with awe. She continues to the far side of the room, but I stay to marvel at the fireplace first, my gaze resting on the massive picture hanging over the mantle. Surprised, I blink before doing a double take. My eyes have not been deceived. The picture is a painting by Salvador Dali, his most famous. Three watches seem to be melting while ants devour a fourth timepiece, and a face in profile appears to be sleeping underneath one of the melting watches on his cheek. It's an odd piece to have hanging in such a place of prominence, even if it is in a secret attic of sorts, and I wonder when it was placed there. If I remember correctly, the original was created in 1931 and was a lot smaller than what I'm standing in front of. I lean in closer to get a better look, but the picture is too high up, and I don't want to fall into the firebox.

Standing back, I take in the picture as a whole and realize it isn't a Dali at all but a really close replica with one vast difference. Here, there is a second person in the picture. The figure is small and almost hidden, much like the fly on the watch. He, or she—I can't tell—stands in front of the cliffs, with hands on either side of the head, the mouth open. I guess Edvard Munch's screamer made it into the picture too. It almost appears as if the person is looking out past the watches on the desert-like landscape and into the room in which we stand. I shiver and reassure myself that I'm not alone up here. Lyn's with me.

"Oh, you found the Dali."

So engrossed in the painting and the story I was imagining in my head, I didn't even hear Hammond come into the room. I jump, and when I turn to face him, his shoulders are shaking with silent laughter.

"I didn't mean to frighten you. I called out to you at the doorway, but you must not have heard me."

"No, I didn't. I'm sorry. Is it really a Dali?

"No. If you look closely, the painting isn't signed. If you ask me, I think the person who built this place created it." Hammond's dark eyes take in the room appraisingly before resting on the painting once more.

Lyn, upon hearing voices, comes over and looks at the painting too. "How old is this place, anyway?" she asks. "Downstairs, I'd guess twenty, thirty years max, but up here, it's like the place is hundreds of years old. Was it renovated downstairs?" Then, changing the subject completely, "I mean, look at the person in the distance. Why even incorporate him or her?"

Hammond ignores Lyn's questions and continues to stare at the picture himself. "What is that in the center, anyway?" he asks, quickly glancing at me before turning back to the painting and pointing to the sleeping mass on the desert floor. When I don't readily answer, he continues. "It looks like an eye to me. See the eyelashes? Seems the artist wanted to emphasize sleep, perhaps allude to the truth we find there. Guess this guy wanted to rest a bit and time got away from him."

Hammond laughs at his own feeble joke and I smile, more from Lyn's snort than from the joke itself. "Anyway, look at everything that's happening around him. That can't happen in real life—melting clocks, weird creatures with huge eyelashes—that's what happens inside." Hammond points to his head. "It's the stuff we create for ourselves to help us figure things out." Hammond glances at me and Lyn before turning back to the portrait. "Maybe that's what the other person in the background is recognizing, that life's lived on the inside more than it is on the outside."

"This place really is about self-reflection and all that, isn't it? This really is a retreat—of sorts." Lyn stares at Hammond, her eyes narrowed, calculating. "I'm sorry . . . about before," she says, and I'm floored by her complete one-eighty. "I understand now." She nods at the pictures. "I just—all of this is frustrating."

Hammond peers down his nose at Lyn and then stares at the picture for a few moments more before clearing his throat.

"We want you to know that we're going to turn off the electricity pretty soon. It won't be off for too long. We have to check on some things. Some of these rooms are quite dark, especially up here with all this stuff, so watch your step." He scans the room once more. I dip my head in understanding and glance at my watch, surprised an hour has already passed since we came up here.

As he walks toward the stairwell, Hammond calls over his shoulder, "Take care. Enjoy yourself." And with that, he disappears down the stairs.

"What am I, chopped liver?" Lyn asks, her hands pulling her hair into a tight ponytail before letting it all go again.

I scrunch my brow. "What are you talking about, and what was all that 'I understand now' crap?" I move toward the pictures to see if I too can gain new insight.

"It's like he was trying to act like I'm not even here, like he was ignoring me. I tried to apologize."

"And I heard that." I pat Lyn's shoulder. "Since when do you care what some old guy, whom you're likely never going to see again after this, thinks, anyway?"

"True." She crosses her arms in front of her. "I'm going to go downstairs, go to the bathroom, and get a sweater or something. I'm cold. Are you okay up here by yourself? We can always come back later."

I grin. "This is my candy store, woman! Go. I'll be fine. I'll try to wrap it up while you're gone."

Lyn shakes her head. "You're so weird," she says gruffly, but I can see her smile before she turns away and heads down the stairs.

Alone, I peruse the portraits and landscape scenes on the wall. Walking up to one, I observe the expressive eyes, the color of the hair, the tilt of the head. And when I move on to regard the next, it's as if I've forgotten what I just looked at. This happens several times before I shake my head to clear it. It's not that I'm not interested, but my shock of waking up here or hangover or whatever it is must have a stronger hold on me than I realized. I can't focus.

I turn away from the wall of pictures and move toward the wall of windows instead. One window, at the far end of the room, is partially uncovered, the curtain rod hanging only by one end, and I can see the glass has a large crack from the bottom center to halfway up one side.

I make my way toward it, moving past an old rocking chair that begins to gently rock, and I'm reminded of the one Lyn and I used to have in our room for ages. For just a moment, my heart aches, and I reach out, the whisper of a smile on my lips. I sometimes wish I could go back and be a kid again. No worries, and what I was going to do and who I was going to play with that day, my only care. It makes me sad for a minute, but I dismiss the thought and move on.

Lyn and I are adults now, and the rocking chair was removed a long time ago. After the accident, the way I thought about the world changed and the way I responded to it did too. Lyn never liked it. "Come on," she would say. "What's happened to you? To us. You are me and I am you, remember?" It was a phrase we'd say when looking at each other. Mirror twins.

Lyn is stronger than me. She can handle what happened to her, and as her attitude attests even now, that strength endures. I, on the other hand, have internalized her wounds, withdrawing in many ways in order to have the strength to continue. I've accepted it.

I have.

We're still close, but it's different. Before, well, we shared everything. There were no secrets. After, it was like this disconnect. It took some time to get used to. I don't remember how many weeks I spent crying myself to sleep every night with the thought that for the sake of my sanity, I had lost a part of myself.

She hasn't come back up yet, but I know she's here in this house with me. I can imagine what I'm sure she would be muttering as I look over all this "junk" she doesn't know why I bother with. It's okay she doesn't like some of what I like.

That she puts up with it despite the fact she doesn't like it makes it special.

The window, for some reason, keeps calling me and I move a couple of boxes out of the way to clear a path. One of the boxes has a lid that slides off onto the floor, and when I pick it up, naturally I take a peek at what's inside.

A whole bunch of swimming trophies meet my gaze. Big ones and little ones, gold, silver, and bronze. Some of them are just medallions hanging on red, white, and blue striped ribbon, while others would proudly sit on shelves. There are a few certificates of achievement in old, tarnished frames waiting to be displayed on a wall. The number of awards and medals is impressive, and from the amount, the recipient must have spent years honing his or her skills.

The weird thing is, on all of them, the name has been scratched out, redacted. I search the box for evidence of a name somewhere, maybe on a piece of paper or on the box itself. Nothing. The person didn't want to forget. Why else have the awards in a box in the attic to begin with? Might as well throw them in the trash and be done with it all. Instead, it's almost as if someone wanted to get rid of the name itself. *Why?*

I think about all the hard work this person went through to achieve so many accolades only to turn away from them, and of course, I think of my own shortcomings when it comes to water. What I wouldn't do for a chance to be out there, unafraid, floating up and down on the waves, the cool water soothing me as the warm sun beats down upon me. It sounds gloriously wonderful, especially the part about not being afraid.

I close the box and move forward. I don't even remember how I became scared of water in the first place. I used to love it as a child. Lyn and I would beg to go to the neighborhood pool during the summer, and when we could get to the lake or the ocean, we would spend hours in the water, our parents, who kept a sharp eye on us, calling us out only to reapply suntan lotion and make sure we weren't getting too tired.

Even now, with my fear, the *sound* of soft waves lightly lapping against the shore is calming, soothing, and it's nothing for me to sit on a beach at a distance from the shore, eyes closed, and soak up the sun and the pacifying timbre of the surf. And typically, if I deem myself far enough away, watching the hypnotizing motion of each swell relaxes me. So *why not today*? I wonder if it has something to do with how I got here.

I tilt my head one way, then the other, allowing my neck to crack. I don't want to think about it. Every time I do, anxiety swells within my breast, and my fight-or-flight reflexes kick in. I don't want to get to the point where I'm sitting in the corner rocking back and forth to soothe myself. I'm here to relax. *Reflect too*, an inner, snarky voice reminds me, and I shut her up quickly by pushing a small table out of my way, its feet dragging on the floorboards, drowning out anything more the voice may want to say.

When I get to the window, I find the roof outside partially obstructing my view. I press my face against the cool glass as if that will help me get a better vantage point. It's silly, I know, but I do it just the same. Finally coming to the easy conclusion that I won't be able to see past the black shingles, I turn to look the other way.

There's the water. Again. Only I can see a dock now too. An empty one. I scrunch my eyebrows. Maybe they have another dock on the other side of the island. Or maybe a boat garage. As I'm thinking, movement catches my eye, and I see someone, a girl or woman—from this distance and angle, it's hard to tell—walk onto the wooden planks and sit on its edge, her feet dangling off the side. She looks back toward the house, and for a moment, I swear she's looking up toward the attic, her eyes searching out mine. I gasp and lean back, not wanting her to see me. I feel like an intruder, trespassing on her thoughts and feelings. It's stupid, I know.

After a minute, I lean forward again and watch her, and I wonder what she's thinking, what *she's* watching. All I can think of is a mirror reflection where you can see yourself viewing yourself over and over again, in smaller and smaller frames.

As I'm thinking this, the creak of the floorboards and a drawn-out sigh announce Lyn's arrival at the top of the stairs.

"Lyn! Come here. There's someone out on the dock."

As I stare out the window at the girl, I hear a crash behind me, and then Lyn swears. My hands rise in front of me reflexively just as Lyn almost falls on top of me, two overturned boxes in her wake.

Instead of looking at the mess she created, Lyn grabs onto my shoulders to steady herself, then peers over my shoulder. "Where?"

"Right there," I say, pointing to the dock, but there's no one there. "Well, someone was just there."

"Girl or guy?"

"Does it matter?" I ask, my eyebrows arched.

Lyn shrugs. "I thought maybe it was this Nick guy we heard about. Wouldn't you like to know what the hell is going on?" She brushes off dust from her jeans. "Or are you just super content to look through the boxes of someone's memories?"

She's got me there. "I'm pretty sure a woman, even though I couldn't really tell much about her from up here. She had long hair, and she was just sitting at the edge of the dock looking out at the water."

I crane my neck, trying to get a better angle from which to see out the window, but it doesn't matter. The woman's gone.

"Are you sure you saw someone?"

"What do you mean, am I sure? I saw her as clearly as I see you, only you're here and she was down there on the dock," I say, nodding my head toward the window and what lay beyond it. "She may not be Nick, but maybe she's the owner Gail and Hammond said was around."

Lyn glances skeptically out the window again. "Well, we could always go down and find out. It would get us out of this place at least," she says, eyeing the room with distaste.

"Yeah, we better go down anyway. They haven't turned off the electricity yet, and it's getting dark." Outside, a very real and very present storm is rising. Dark, menacing clouds advance toward the house, threatening streaks of lightning, and upon seeing the approaching shadows, my ears are finally open to the growl of thunder and the tap, tap, tapping of a tree branch demanding sanctuary from what looks like will be a torrential downpour. "It's going to storm."

Lyn whistles. "Maybe that's why ghost girl disappeared."

"She wasn't a ghost. She was right there."

"I'm messing with you. Come on." Lyn swivels and makes her way across the expanse, not even bothering to pretend to try to pick up the boxes she tipped over.

I roll my eyes and sigh. Loudly.

"What? It's just a bunch of stuff in an attic. If they wanted it on display, it would be downstairs, don't you think?"

"If they wanted it tossed around instead of packed away, they would have tossed it around, don't you think?" I counter. "Just go," I say as I start for the overturned boxes. "I'll clean this up and be right behind you."

I don't have to tell her twice. She's bounding down the stairs without so much as a backward glance. "Hurry up," she calls up to me from the bottom as if I'm the one who tipped them over. "I'll go and look for Nick or ghost girl downstairs."

I flip the boxes over and start stuffing their contents inside, not even bothering to examine the treasures someone else has packed so meticulously. She pisses me off when she acts like I'm here to clean up her messes. It's no use arguing with her though, because it'll go in one ear and out the other.

It's my behavior that has to change. I know this, so maybe she's not the one who pisses me off.

Maybe it's me.

Right as I'm cramming the last of the items into the second box, they turn off the electricity. *Great.* Hammond said it wasn't going to be for long, but I really don't want to stay up here, by myself, and wait for it to come back on, especially now that the black clouds must be right on top of the house. It's almost as dark as night, and the grimy window, the one not covered, isn't letting in nearly enough light for my liking.

I stand up with the box and put it on top of the other one, which I can just make out before I turn toward where the stairs are located. All I can do is inch my way forward, moving around the boxes and furniture I come across in my path.

Suddenly, from behind me, I hear something scrape against the floorboards. It's just a whisper of noise, but it's made all the louder in what now seems like a closed space filled with dust and cobwebs and shrouded mysteries. For a second, I consider ignoring it, just running toward the staircase, any boxes or furniture I trip over be damned. I know it's probably my imagination; it has to be, but it doesn't stop me from turning sharply anyway, my heart beating madly in my chest as I search for the source of the sound.

My sight abruptly sharpens, and even though it's still quite dark, I imagine I see shadows on the wall that shift when my eyes flicker away from them and the rocking chair I bumped into earlier moving by itself even with the absence of a breeze. Shivering, I start toward the stairs once again, and I swallow to try to slow my breath, which is coming out in ragged pants.

I'm determined not to scream. *It's just my imagination.* I think about Lyn's words, "ghost girl," and my throat tightens. This is ridiculous. I'm in an attic; no more, yet I find myself moving faster, wondering how the hell the attic can all of a sudden seem to be twice, no, three times the size it was when I came up here and feel so cramped at the same time.

A large armoire blocks my way and I move around it, my heart coming to a standstill.

My hand comes up to stop a scream.

She stands in front of me, her hair in her face, and for a moment, not even a fraction of a second, it looks like she has been caught in the storm outside, her hair plastered to her cheeks, her eyes wide as her hand, too, goes up to stifle a scream.

I step back at the same time she does, and that's when I let out a shaky but relieved puff of air.

A mirror. It's a freaking mirror.

She is me, and I am her. Ha. In this case, ain't it the truth.

## Chapter 5

When I get to the bottom step, I breathe a sigh of relief. The mirror startled me, but being up in the attic itself is a source of inspiration. There are so many memories stuffed into boxes and piled on the floor, and it makes me want to nose my way into all the rooms to take a look, get a feel for the person who lives here. Gail and Hammond said owner. Singular. One person living all alone in such a big house.

I walk up three steps to the hall where my room is located. Lyn should be somewhere around here too, and I wonder if she is in her room or wandering a different part of the house looking for Nick as she said she would.

Moving down the hall, I can see that most of the doors are closed now. I could just glance into those that are ajar—to find Lyn, of course. One door, about two doors down from mine, is filled with all things for a young child. A crib lines one wall with three or four crocheted blankets draped over the side. I can picture some doting mother or grandmother knitting away when hearing of the upcoming birth. A playpen sits kitty-corner from it and inside are a bunch of toys, including wooden blocks, those colorful, stackable plastic rings, and a tiny xylophone. There are a couple of strollers folded up and lying on the floor and a changing table lining the other wall. Lotions and plastic boxes stick out from under it as if waiting for the baby to come back.

But I don't think the baby *is* coming back. I open the door farther and step inside. Everything has the air of disuse. It's not that everything is dusty like up in the attic, but everything looks as if it has already been used and then just discarded. The gauzy curtain over the window doesn't help. With the already somber light coming in, the filmy cover only enhances the quality of abandonment.

I walk to the partially opened louvered doors of a closet and peek inside. Clothes for a little girl, ranging from newborn to two or three years old, hang from a rack halfway down the wall. Some outfits are pristine, like they've only been worn once if at all, and others look well-loved with stains and patches. Above the clothes, a shelf lined with scuffed baby shoes ranging in size reminds me of memory boxes filled with bronzed little shoes and baby handprints preserved in clay.

I look at the crib once more. What is the point of keeping all this stuff down here? Why not free up the space and keep this stuff up in the attic with everything else?

With the electricity out and the room growing darker by the minute, there is no point trying to continue my snooping. I should look for Lyn. Sighing, I give a final look around me when a noise by the door makes me jump. I'm sure my eyes are as big as those of a deer caught in the headlights until I see Lyn's form glide past.

I call out to her and then rush to the door to get her attention, ready to gossip about why all this stuff is kept here when there clearly is no baby on the premises. But when I get to the door, I realize it's not Lyn. The woman is facing away from me, just standing there as if she's waiting for something, and although she looks like Lyn from the back, there is something distinctly *not* Lyn about her stance. Instinctively, I slouch back into the doorway, tempted to speak and have her turn around but at the same time, afraid of what I'll see. I imagine her face will be skeletal, her eyes sunken and staring menacingly at me, or she'll be hideously disfigured or something.

"Lyn?" I squeak because although I know it's not Lyn, she doesn't know I don't know.

The girl tilts her head, and her hair, which appears wet in the darkened hall, tilts to the side as well. I can tell she heard me, but instead of a nice, "Yes, can I help you?" or even a "What the hell do you want?" she just continues to stand, facing away, any movement she makes awkward and stiff. She lifts her foot, planning to walk away, but I try again.

"Wait. Are you the owner?"

Her head tilts back so that it's straight once more, and I brace myself. My heart is beating fast, and I know that if she turns, even slightly, I'll most likely run in the opposite direction without looking back. I don't know what it is. Most likely I've freaked myself out by imagining her as a mutilated corpse, but there's something about the storm and how she's dripping onto the wood floors. The fact I'm standing in the doorway of a room full of abandoned baby items makes the whole situation eerie beyond words.

Again, she lifts her foot, and this time I remain silent.

She continues forward, slowly at first, and then as if getting her stride, she moves more quickly. When she reaches the end of the hallway, she turns and disappears around the corner.

My breath coming too quickly, I raise my hand to my chest. My heart is pounding, my eyes are wide, and my hands are shaking. One would think I would turn around and find

Lyn immediately. But no. I'm the girl in the horror flicks running up the stairs instead of running out the front door, the girl who picks up the stranger in the middle of nowhere after hearing there is a maniac on the loose killing everyone in his path, and in this particular case . . . yeah, I'm the one who follows the creepy dripping girl like the idiot I am.

Small drops of water on the floor shine in the dim light coming from windows in the rooms with opened doors, letting me know she isn't a figment of my imagination. As I stalk down the hall, I'm silent, my eyes down, my senses on high alert. Everything is altogether too quiet for my liking. All I can think is that she's waiting for me just around the corner, waiting to rake her fingernails down my face or hack me to pieces with a machete she's pulled from thin air.

So, I prepare myself. Right as I get to the corner, I take a deep breath and then I jump.

"Agghhhh!" I yell.

"Agghhhh!" returns Hammond before he immediately starts sputtering and choking. A water glass smashes on the floor, and shards of glass and a spray of water fly in all directions.

"Oh! Oh, Hammond. I'm so sorry!" I go to pat him on the back, but he waves me away, glaring at me while he continues to cough.

"You want to tell me what you think you were doing?" he demands through gasps as he registers the mess of glass and the puddle on the floor.

"I saw someone walk this way, and I followed . . ." It sounds lame even to me. What was I planning to do if the girl had been around this corner anyway? She clearly didn't want to talk, or she would have said something. And it's not like it's any of my business what she's doing here either.

"Let me get that for you," I say and immediately squat when I see Hammond bend to pick up the glass.

"No!" Hammond yells. Then, more quietly, "No. There's no need." He coughs some more. "Just—" He puts his fingers to his head as if he's got a major headache—of which I'm most likely the cause—and coughs again. "Just go and relax. I'll get this."

I pick up a few shards, ready to go against Hammond's wishes, but he puts his hand on my arm and shakes his head before taking the shards one by one from my hand. He then points toward the way I had come.

"Hammond, did you see someone—besides me, I mean—walking down the hall?"

His eyes are almost black as he stares at me intently, and I'm sorry I even asked. I hesitate a moment more before standing and open my mouth to apologize again, but the words don't come. Instead, I watch him take out a handkerchief to use for gathering the shards.

I'm about to walk away when he mutters, "I've only seen you." I wait for more or for him to look at me again, but he doesn't, and when things can't possibly get any more uncomfortable, I turn and head for the stairs.

➤ The House on the Lake

## Chapter 6

Something pulls me out of my reverie and momentarily lost, I look around me. I'm on an enclosed porch on one side of the manor. After leaving Hammond to clean up the glass I made him drop, I came downstairs and walked out the front door. I needed fresh air. The wind had been blowing the rain right up to the front door, but I had noticed this porch, connected by a door, and decided to check it out.

I remember sitting. I remember thinking how pretty the room is, and then I remember wondering for the umpteenth time how the hell I managed to get on an island, not to mention why I don't remember signing up for a retreat in the first place.

Tapping my hand against my thigh and sighing, I stand and look around the room. It's cozy despite all the windows. A large rectangular rug lies on the floor and unlike the light colors I've seen a lot of inside, this room is dark, like the halls. The rug is black, the two-seater and three-seater wicker couches dark gray, and the pillows are a mixture of vibrant reds, oranges, and dark blues all in a jumble of chaotic waves.

I don't know how long I've been in here, but the storm is over. Through some trees on the grounds, I can see an expanse of dark water twinkling and blinking in the sunlight, and when I look up, only a few clouds mar the light blue sky. I didn't fall asleep. I know that, which means I must have zoned out.

Forgetting what pulls me from what I'm doing in the first place is troublesome though. I don't like being unable to account for missing time, and that's the only thing that has me upset about the retreat. If I can remember how I got here, I'll rest easier, be able to relax.

And that's another thing. I said it was a rare occurrence, this whole zoning out thing, but considering the huge chunk of time concerning my arrival that's missing, frequency is becoming an issue. A little Google session might be in order when I find my phone.

I glance out the window again, hoping it will give me a straw to grasp as to what I was thinking.

Nothing. All I see is the water I've been trying to forget.

I cock my head toward a faint sound of laughter to listen more carefully. Lyn's and that of a man's. Hammond? I smile and give a sniff of amusement as I continue toward the sound coming from the exposed porch connected to this one. I really shouldn't be surprised she's won him over, especially given the fact that I almost drowned the poor guy in a swallow of water.

As I open the enclosed porch door, the laughter is louder, and when I get to the source, I'm surprised. It's not Hammond's at all. Instead, it's that of a much younger man— tall, attractive—if his profile is anything to go by, and looking toward the dock, he's apparently the owner of a boat.

Lyn sees me first and lifts her hand in a wave. "Eve, come here! This is Phoenix Anker. He's the one Gail and Hammond told us about."

He stands with the sun at his back as I move down the porch steps, so it shadows his face as I walk toward him, but at least it also hides the water behind him. I have to shield my eyes until I get up close, and when I do, all I can think of is what my face must look like, all scrunched up in trying to see. He grasps my shoulders, turning me so I'm standing in his shadow, his body blocking the sun. His eyes, the most spectacular color green I've ever seen, light up with amusement as he smiles at me. I've never been one to get too wrapped up in a person's looks, but for a few moments, I make an exception. I'm struck not only by his eyes but by the sheer magnetism that's oozing off him. He's broad-shouldered and his torso tapers down to a trim waist. I wouldn't call him sexy exactly, but he has an appeal that heats my blood and makes me want to lean into his touch.

He releases my shoulders. "Please, call me Nick. You're Eve?" I'm not ready to talk yet, but I'm capable of nodding, and he takes that as a sign to continue. "Lyn was telling me about how you came to be here. You don't remember anything?"

Sheepishly, I shake my head. "It's pretty embarrassing, I know. All I can think is that I either knocked my head or blocked it all out." Nick looks to Lyn, confusion written on his face.

"Eve's afraid of water," she supplies for me. I wonder if she's mentioned that she doesn't remember getting here either.

"It's true." I turn to Nick as if he'll be able to provide the necessary answers, and he eyes both of us as if trying to decipher that same conundrum.

"So, you believe you're supposed to be here," he says, looking at me, "and you don't," he finishes, looking at Lyn.

Behind him, the sky remains mostly clear and bright. It's hard to believe there has been a storm here at all, and although the yard looks a bit ravaged from the wind and rain, the shore is completely clear of all debris, and the water continues to sparkle under the sunshine.

"Well, I think it's absolutely beautiful here. It's a wonderful place for a retreat."

"I told you, Eve loves the house," said Lyn with a knowing smirk. "It's a bit lonely and a bit too, um, different, for my taste, but it's right up Eve's alley."

Nick's looking at the house behind me, his nod the only indication he has heard anything Lyn said. The way he seems to come to himself and smile at the two of us has me wondering if he has taken in what she was saying or is merely responding to the absence of her voice. He gives us a harried smile. "It's definitely got its charm, every house does, but all the way out here? I'd rather be out there—" He points to the lake, but I know he means what's beyond it. "John Donne once said, 'no man is an island' and I choose to take that literally."

I smile even though it feels as though I need to show him around, defend the place I'm calling home for the next few days. He must see something in my eyes because his soften. He scans the grounds and the house and sighs. "To be honest, I haven't been here in ages. My family owns a lot of houses, and as long as we know things are running smoothly, we tend to let people get on." He doesn't say it with arrogance, just as a matter of fact, so I don't bristle at his words. "You said you are here for a retreat?"

At that moment, Gail appears at the front door, her hands bunched in front of her as usual, and looks at Nick pointedly. "Mr. Anker! I thought I heard you. May I have a word with you for a moment, please?"

She steps outside onto the big wooden porch that stretches the length of the house. When Nick bounds up the steps, she grasps his forearm firmly, guiding him several feet away, her head angled toward his.

He nods as she talks, and his eyes swing over to me and then Lyn. Whoops, caught in the act of trying to eavesdrop. Quickly, I look away, blushing.

As Nick leans into Gail and hurriedly whispers something, Lyn moves closer. "What do you think they're talking about? Told you we're not supposed to be here."

"Maybe," I respond, taking a worried peek at Gail and Nick. I hope we're allowed to be here, that he lets us stay. "He didn't seem to know about the retreat. I'm sure I have the confirmation number and paperwork somewhere. It's not like me to forget something like that."

"No, it's not like you to forget. You usually remember everything. It's annoying." Lyn rolls her eyes. "Anyway, when

I saw his boat pull up, the only thing I could think was that we're saved, so I have no qualms about leaving now."

Nick says something else to Gail, and when she doesn't respond right away, he puts his hands on her shoulders and bends so that he is looking her straight in the eyes. Either he's trying to intimidate her or he's giving her a pep talk, and I hate that I can't see which it is from this angle.

When Gail nods, Nick straightens and heads in our direction.

"I'm sorry about that. It seems I wasn't filled in on all the aspects of your stay with us."

"I—I'm sorry! Are we not supposed to be here? I just—how could we get rooms? And Gail said—"

"No, no. I'm sorry. You have nothing to worry about, Eve. You're welcome here any time. Really. We just can't account for, well . . ." He looks back to where Gail was standing, but she's no longer there, having disappeared back into the house. "Listen, don't worry about it. Not important."

Noticing my reticence, Nick laughs and holds out his hand. "Maybe we should start over. Hi, I'm Nick Anker. Welcome to Lakeview Manor."

I grasp his hand and shake it firmly, noting that he appears satisfied when I do. He repeats the gesture with Lyn.

"A good handshake shows strength," Nick says, looking at us each in turn. "Mentally and physically, and that's always good to have, right?" He claps his hands together before holding one hand in front of him, palm up in a lead-the-way signal. "Shall we?" he says as he moves up the stairs once more, toward some golden-toned wicker chairs with cream-colored cushions.

"So," Nick says as he makes himself comfortable in one chair, "what have they told you about Lakeview? Sorry. As I said, my family owns a lot of houses, so sometimes things happen, and I'm not aware of what's going on because . . . well, because life, if that makes sense."

"Yeah, that makes perfect sense," I say, taking a seat as well and watching him as he stretches his legs out in front of him. They're nice legs even if he is wearing slacks so I can't see them as clearly as I'd like. "There's not much to tell. I don't really remember everything, which makes me sound like a complete idiot, I know." My hands grasp each other as I try to remember. "I must have the papers somewhere." My eyes narrow as I focus on a memory. "I remember, 'relax, reflect, and release'. Those words. I found this place in an article or online or something." I scratch my head, trying to remember the details. "It said remote location, something, something, retreat . . . and I wanted to come and check the place out because it sounded so mysterious. I remember asking for more details, but honestly, I don't remember getting a response. But I must have, right? I mean, I know I'm here for a week.

"Gail and Hammond have been great though, very accommodating. They said they knew my name, so I figure I was expected, but they also said they were busy and weren't around when I got here, so they haven't been able to help much." Nick watches me, his eyes narrowed in thought, and Lyn is staring at her shoes, but I can tell she's listening as well and probably wondering how she fits into all of this.

"You're on the Isle of Esse," Nick states as he crosses his ankles and leans back in his chair. "As you can see, it's a pretty small island located in the middle of nowhere." Nick smiles. "I shouldn't say that, really. The mainland is not too far away. It's about a ten-minute boat ride." I raise my head toward the water. I find it hard to believe. I don't see any land besides the land on which the house sits. Of course, I haven't been around the entire island either, so perhaps I can see it from the other side of the house.

"Wait, we're on the Isle of Esse? I don't remember seeing that the retreat was located here, but I've heard of this place. I've always wanted to come here."

Nick's eyebrows raise. "You have?"

"You have?" Lyn echoes. "Why is this the first time I'm hearing about it?"

I glare at her and then shrug. She acts like I'm supposed to tell her every aspect of what's going on. And maybe *always* wanting to come here is an exaggeration. I frown.

From what I remember, Lakeview Manor *is* legendary, even though I didn't realize the retreat I signed up for was *the* manor I heard about. The story goes that people have always been fascinated with its history, but no one knows exactly what it is. It changes. Ask one person, and what he has heard from his neighbor's sister's cousin will be completely different from what someone else heard from his mother, whose friend's nephew went. But one of the most interesting things for me is that I know no one personally who has ever been. It's always a friend of a friend, or there is some convoluted relationship to the person who went. No one I know has ever seen it with their own eyes. There aren't even any pictures. There is so much mystery and intrigue surrounding the place that now that I know where I am, I can't wait to continue exploring once again.

I look at Nick. "Up until now, I thought this place was a myth. All anybody can do is imagine what this place is like, and here we are. It's a once-in-a-lifetime opportunity."

From the corner of my eye, I can see Lyn rolling hers. She's the type to live in the moment. I'm not saying she's reckless, but she'd much rather jump in the pool before learning how to swim, and I . . . well, I'd stay on the shore. Far, far back. But I almost smirk with glee when I see her take a surreptitious peek around, most likely wondering if maybe she has underestimated the manor.

Nick, on the other hand, seems to consider my words. "For most people, I guess you're right." He taps his fingers on his chair and glances toward the pier where the boat he came in sits gently rocking on the waves. "You know, I realize this place is here, I know it's spectacular—as you've just verified—and I understand there's a lot this place can offer, but it's never been a place I've particularly felt the need to visit. It sits here on its pretty little island, not making waves, and besides general maintenance, I've never had to worry about it." His eyes widen. "It's not that I've neglected it. I don't want you to think that! It's great. I love it, but there has been some disuse over the last several years, and sometimes homes just need a bit more time, and a little more TLC. So, I'm glad you're here."

I feel my cheeks heating and all of a sudden, the lake seems to need all my attention. "Thank you," I manage.

"There's a lot to take in here. It's—" I shake my head "—I have no words. And you own it!"

"Well, I personally don't own it, but I manage it . . . Me and my brother." Nick's smile disappears, and he abruptly has an interest in the wooden floorboards. Lyn must not notice because when she hears *brother,* her ears perk up. It's not because Nick is talking about another man either. This would have been Lyn's reaction had he said sister. She loves meeting people and getting to know all about them. It's not fake either. She genuinely enjoys it, and even though I can see Nick has become uncomfortable, Lyn just sees a new avenue of questioning.

"Oooh, brothers!" She nudges me with her elbow and wiggles her eyebrows. "Are we going to get to meet him, and is he as handsome as you?"

"I guess some people are attracted to him, but I'm pretty sure they're just desperate."

"Whoa! That was harsh!" Lyn says, laughing, and I see a smile tug at the corner of Nick's mouth. "What's wrong with him? Or is it that you're jealous?

"Jealous?" Nick harrumphs. "Hardly. Listen, I'd rather not talk about my brother if you don't mind, but . . ." Nick glances at me and then back to Lyn. "If you see him, you might want to keep your distance."

It's not exactly what someone wants to hear when they are on an island. I reach out and touch Nick's arm; then I wait for him to look me in the eye. "Should we be afraid?"

Nick sighs before muttering, "Most people are when they meet him."

"Wait, what?" I lean forward in my chair. "Why? Is he dangerous?"

Nick sticks his hands in his pockets and pulls out keys on a ring with a charm attached. It looks like a cross on the top part, but the bar above the cross is shaped like a teardrop. Clearly unwilling to talk about what he just stated, he fiddles with the charm. For a moment, he looks like a petulant child—albeit a cute one.

"You have to give us something, Nick," Lyn says. "You can't just spring something like that on a person and then expect them to act as if it has never been said, especially if there's the possibility of us running into him." She's silent for a moment, letting her words sink in. Then she repeats my question. "Is he dangerous?"

Nick scowls and focuses on the charm and even on individual keys. When he can't find enough to interest him there, his attention turns to the lake. Lyn turns to me with questions in her eyes. I shrug and shake my head, but I scooch my chair closer to hers. If there's a dangerous man on the island, then I'll be damned if we're going to stay on the island too. Fear of the water or not.

Lyn starts to rise from her chair. "Maybe we should go and get—"

"No, okay?" Nick cuts in, and he takes a moment to level his gaze with each of us. "No, I can't say he's dangerous."

"But you said people are afraid when they meet him. Why? What is there to be afraid of?" I ask.

"It's nothing. Forget I said anything." Noting the concern on both Lyn's face and mine, he sighs. "I'm being petty. No, he wouldn't hurt you; he's not dangerous. He's . . . there's just been this thing between us for a long time."

For the most part, I'm cautious by nature, but Nick's error was in dangling a mystery in front of my face—even if only between brothers—and then snatching it away. Now, I'm intrigued. He's informed us there's no danger, and he's also said people are afraid of his brother. Now, there's the mystery of Lakeview and perhaps a mystery of the brothers to solve. Who is this brother, and how is he different from the one seated before me?

Lyn nudges me. "We'll go. Right?" She nods without even regarding me, as if it's the only reasonable conclusion. "I mean, he's got a boat, and he can take us back—" She glances at Nick. "You will take us back, right?"

"Yes, I can take you right now." Nick nods, shoves the keys he was fiddling with back into his pocket, and rises from the chair quickly. "If you want, I can help you grab your stuff. I—"

"Is your brother even here?" I ask while still seated. Although he seems like a nice enough guy, his actions since I've met him lead me to suspect he's not being completely honest about everything—his whispers with Gail, the way he talks about his brother. "Lyn and I haven't seen anyone besides Gail and Hammond on the island until you came. And we haven't seen any other boats unless there's another dock somewhere."

I leave out seeing the woman on the dock because . . . well, I don't know why I leave her out. Maybe because I'm scared Lyn is right and what I saw was a ghost or a figment of my imagination. The way she moved and then disappeared around the corner . . . Lyn eyes me sharply and frowns at my leaving "ghost girl" out, so I know there will be some explaining on my part later, but right now, I'm just grateful she doesn't say anything about her either.

Regardless, I feel as if my hand is being forced, like Nick and Lyn are trying to take me from a place I find extraordinarily comfortable, and it may be under Nick's management, but he said I will always be welcome here, that he was glad I was here, and right now, that's what I want more than anything. As for Lyn, she may have been with me all my life, but it doesn't mean I have to follow her lead on everything.

"I'm sorry. I don't mean to be rude, but unless you're telling me to leave. I'd like to stay. Is that a problem?"

## Chapter 7

Nick's eyes widen. "No, not at all!" he says. He rakes his fingers through his sandy hair, then rubs his temples. "I seem to keep putting my foot in my mouth today. I'm sorry."

Lyn looks from Nick to me and back again. "You can take us back whenever we want?"

"Of course. That's all I meant to offer."

"Are you sure, Eve?" Lyn jumps out of her seat and moves away from Nick, beckoning me to follow. When I do, she leans toward me and whispers, "What are you doing? We can leave right now! I know you like this sort of thing, but come back another time when you actually remember signing up for the place!"

I shake my head. I want to stay. I need to stay. It's like this place is calling for me to figure out its secrets. And anyway, I'm already here. "I don't want to go." I can feel my excitement growing as I look at Lyn. "Do you know how many people dream about coming back from this place with answers to its mysteries? The Isle of Esse. Can you believe it?

And we're here!" Lyn bites her lip and looks down. "You can go if you want," I assure her. "And you know where I am, so it's all good."

Lyn sighs. I can tell she's torn. I know there's a part of her that longs to explore and see what's going on under the surface of the place. I watch the play of emotions on her face: frustration, confusion, indecision, curiosity. Finally, she nudges past me and walks back over to Nick.

"We're going to stay a little longer," she says, giving me a glare. "Maybe Eve will remember some stuff. I don't think this retreat is too long anyway. It isn't, is it?" she asks, ice in her gaze even though her voice holds warmth.

I wince. She's staying for me. I feel a little guilty, but only a little. She had a chance to leave. She still can. "A week." I smile.

"Just a week?" Nick asks, and I wonder if he can feel the tension between Lyn and me. "This place will keep you busy then," he says.

Lyn and I stay quiet. A battle of wills. She wants me to say something, apologize maybe, or suddenly declare I want to leave. I won't. *And what do I want from her?* The question pops into my head and gives me pause. I'm not sure at the moment. It's another mystery I'll have to solve.

Nick clears his throat. "Uh, do you want to go for a quick ride around the lake? The weather is holding up, and the water is calm. I can point out the mainland, show you it's not so hard to get back, and maybe it might even jog your memory."

"I don't really feel up to it right now," I say, casting him a glance. "But if you guys want to go, feel free."

Lyn pulls me to the side once again with a quick smile at Nick. "Are you sure you don't want to come? I'm totally fine with knocking you over the head to get you into the boat." Her lips twitch. She may still be upset, but she's letting it go. I snort. "Seriously," she continues, "I feel like I'm deserting you by leaving you here. You trust him, right? I mean, you don't get the feeling he's going to try to throw me off the boat or anything, do you?"

Surprise courses through me. "No! Lyn!" We may have only just met, but I don't get that type of vibe off Nick at all. We've gotten some mixed signals, but I don't think he's out to intentionally harm us. "Don't even talk like that. I—" I arch my brows, realizing too late that she was joking. "Ha. Ha. Very funny."

Lyn grins. She can hold her own if she needs to. She holds a green belt in Krav Maga self-defense, so if Nick does try anything, he'll most likely be the one going over the side of the boat. "And what the hell is with that 'Eve can't remember,' crap? I thought you can't remember either."

Lyn refuses to meet my gaze. "Well, maybe I'm starting to remember bits and pieces too," she says. I'm in the middle of puzzling that out when she says, "You don't mind if I go?"

"Why would I mind?" I ask, but I do . . . and she knows it. And the thing is, I don't even know why I mind. The only thing I can put my finger on is that this is my retreat, and already it's been ruined because she is here. Not ruined exactly, but she's not supposed to be here, and now that she is, I feel like I have to cater to her in some way, make time for her, make sure she's okay. I shouldn't have to do that, but I've always done it, ever since the accident at least, and before that, I don't even remember anymore.

Before she can say anything else and before I can get my feelings in order enough to understand my sudden bout of jealousy, I wave to Nick and turn my back to them both. "Just go. It's fine," I say, loud enough for Lyn to hear me.

They're right behind me on the steps, and as I turn left to check out the side of the manor, Lyn and Nick make their way to the boat. I'm envious. I know I don't have Lyn to blame for it. I should be happy she's giving me space. I don't even know why I do it. The excuse is the water today, but

I've made excuses before, taken a back seat when I should have been more out there . . .

I hear their shoes on the dock and watch them step into the boat. Lyn practically jumps on board and Nick uses one of the seats as a step but does it so effortlessly, it's obvious he's been around water all his life.

"We'll be about a half-hour or so," Nick shouts over to me as he unravels the rope from the cleat to which the boat is anchored.

I wave again, then yell at them to have fun and be careful. Lyn waves back as Nick reverses the boat until it has cleared the dock. Then they're racing away. Lyn yelps as she's forced back into the seat with the speed, and there are smiles on both of their faces.

And I'm left to figure out exactly what happened and why I'm peeved. I sit on the front steps and look out at the lake, watching the ripples of water left in the wake of the boat reach out and tap the dock and the shore before retreating once again.

Lyn's not supposed to be here. It was obvious when Gail was saying it was all highly irregular, and that point was driven home when Nick looked a bit perplexed himself. This morning, although disoriented and scared, there was a part of me that felt unfettered, free to take in the experience for what it was with no expectations of how I should act or think or feel. Free to be me.

It's not that I can't be myself around Lyn. I can, but she knows who I am, and sometimes, I just want the freedom to be me without anyone having preconceived ideas of how I should act or be. I want to be able to surprise myself without having to answer for it, and that's the thing. I know Lyn would question everything, and I know I can't fault her because I would do the same.

Then there is Nick. He's attractive and usually when there is an attractive man and Lyn is around, she's the one they are attracted to. It's not that Lyn and I look that different from one another—we're asymmetrically identical—but our personalities are definitely enough to identify us. Whereas Lyn is usually smiling and outgoing, unafraid to ask questions and get to know people, I'm more pensive and quieter, more inclined to stay by myself until I am comfortable with a situation.

Lyn once told me I am afraid to live. She says I need to take chances, stretch my wings, and sometimes I wonder if I would be that type of person if she wasn't always there to be the one to spread *her* wings first.

Anyway, Nick and Lyn appear to be alike when it comes to personalities. The easy laughter I heard before showing myself allowed me to see that. Lyn has that open, come what may attitude, something I envy, and I wonder if Nick is the same.

Drawing in a deep breath, I sigh. My eyes wander over the front yard, from where the front porch ends to where the shore begins. It has flooded before, and puddles still litter the yard from the most recent storm. The shore is only about twenty feet away, and—

I stare at the water and contemplate how I'm feeling. There's no fear. My heartbeat is regular, my breathing natural. *How is this possible?*

Standing, I take a tentative step toward the lake. My heart rate increases, but the usual overwhelming need to run is absent. I take another step, not too big, and think. I was farther away from the house when I was introduced to Nick. *At least to there.* My eyes narrow in on a patch of grass about six feet from where I now stand, and I will myself to walk that far again.

I hear the revving of an engine and look up to spy Nick and Lyn as the boat speeds in the opposite direction from where they headed earlier. They're not ready to come back yet, and Lyn waves as Nick honks the horn, speeding off once again.

My feet are sensitive to the prickly grass. I can feel it through the thin, worn soles of my sandals as I walk parallel to the lake, trying to retain the loose grasp of power I have on my fear. I turn away from the water to stare at the house, anything to keep me from focusing on the water and potentially reigniting my urge to get away.

The house is enormous, impressive, a traditional design with a big, open porch with overhanging beams. A mixture of beige and gray stone and stucco, the house stands three stories high, and when I walk to the corner and look down the side of the house, the side without the enclosed porch I sat in earlier, I can see it's at least as long as it is wide.

A noise catches my attention, and my head snaps toward the sound. Through bushes off to the side of the house, a man with dark hair emerges. He has his hands behind his back and he's so focused on his thoughts, I'm afraid to make a sound for fear of startling him. Whether I unintentionally make a noise, or he just happens to glance up, our eyes lock. From this distance, I can't tell what color his eyes are, but it doesn't matter. His stare is penetrating, and I instinctively bring my arms up to cover myself or ward him off—I can't tell which. He nods, breaking whatever spell I'm under, and gives a small smile. When I mimic him, his smile broadens, but he doesn't move toward me. Instead, he nods once more and walks into the house through a side entrance.

Once he's out of my sight, I shudder, recoiling as if I've just encountered something hideous instead of the gorgeous specimen I've just seen. Could it have been the brother Nick warned us about? His words from when I asked if we should be afraid come back to me: *Most people are when they meet him.* I shudder again. How odd. But my mind reflects on his smile, his wide shoulders, and his confident stride. There was something . . . dangerous about him, a pull I'm strangely willing to explore if I happen to meet him again, which I'm hoping I will.

The rumbling of a boat motor drawing closer yanks me out of my thoughts, and I watch as Nick slows the boat down before he maneuvers it next to the dock once more. I glance at the side door, harboring a hope that the mystery man is there looking back at me and praying that if we do meet again, it will be before his path crosses with Lyn's.

I watch as Nick steps out of the boat and offers his hand to her. She takes it, and I notice how she doesn't immediately let go. Their laughter reaches me before they do.

"Hey! Look at you!" Lyn says as she runs toward me. "I wouldn't have thought you'd get so close by yourself."

I'm pleased she noticed and preen a little before her words have me focusing on just how close I am to the water's edge. The proximity of the lake becomes too much. The glittering waves make my stomach roll, and the fear that eluded me for a good thirty minutes comes back in, well, in waves.

I turn sharply, forcing myself to take a casual stride toward the house. If Lyn notices, she decides to keep it to herself, and for that I'm grateful. "Did you have fun?"

"Yes! Oh, Eve, the mainland isn't too far at all, and Nick says he can take us back whenever we want to go. He says he needs to assess the house for his client, so he'll be around more than he usually is. Isn't that great?"

My run-in with Nick's brother and the whole water incident—no, the whole damn day in general—has left me confused and tired, so I smile and agree with her.

"You know," Nick says, looking from Lyn to me, "I was wondering if you would like to go out to lunch the day after tomorrow. There's this really good restaurant on the mainland I'd love to show you."

I wait to hear Lyn's answer and turn to her expectantly, but Nick is looking at me. His eyes aren't as captivating as his brother's, and his smile, though sincere, doesn't have me feeling like I'd follow him anywhere just to have it shine on me once more. I almost miss his words. "I'm asking you both," he says, and I feel my face heat.

"Sure," I say as I peek at Lyn to see her reaction. If anything, she seems happy I've accepted, and she nods in agreement before confirming herself.

"Absolutely."

"Great! Day after tomorrow it is, then." He rubs his hands together, and he seems genuinely pleased we've both agreed. "Well, I will leave you two to whatever it is that relaxes you. I have some business I have to attend to." Nick heads toward the boat once more, and I call out.

"Why aren't you staying here? There seems to be more than enough room."

"Lakeview Manor is not the only, uh, property I have to look after, and to tell you the truth, I don't want to chance running into my brother." Nick continues to walk toward the boat while twisting his neck so we can hear him. "I'll be back the day after tomorrow to take you out to lunch though. Promise."

As before, Nick steps into the boat so casually, it's as if he was born to it. He starts the engine, backs the boat past the dock, and then waving to us once, he revs the motor and leaves.

Lyn looks at me, grinning. "Well, that was fun."

➤ The House on the Lake

## Chapter 8

"**A**re we going to talk about it?

"Talk about what?" I bend down and pick up a stone, which I carefully inspect in order to avoid Lyn's gaze. We're once again on the porch steps, trying to take advantage of the afternoon light. It's growing dark, and another storm has taken up residence in the east and is slowly making its way toward the island.

"Don't play stupid, Eve. You know what I'm talking about. I've given you your space, allowed you to process, but it's not going to magically go away. How the hell did we get on this island? Why don't you remember?"

"I don't know. Why the hell don't *you* remember?"

"I mean, I guess I can kind of understand. You must have blocked it out or something on the way over, but what about me? I'm not afraid of water. You saw me out there. I enjoyed every minute of it."

"What do you want me to say? You want me to all of a sudden come up with some plausible explanation? I'm sorry,

I can't. And what about you? Why do I get the sneaky suspicion you know exactly what's going on but are refusing to let me in on it?"

Lyn opens her mouth to say something but then mutters something under her breath.

"What was that?" I ask, turning to look her in the eye. "You want to fill me in? Because ever since I woke up this morning, things have been anything but normal. You seemed to think so too, screaming the way you did at Gail and Hammond, making this huge fuss about not remembering, and now you act as if everything is just an inconvenience, that it's my fault because *I* can't remember. What the hell, Lyn?"

"This has happened before, you know."

"That was a long time ago," I say, knowing she's talking about the accident.

"How long did it take you to remember then? A day? Two?"

My smile is saccharine. "I don't remember."

Lyn sighs in exasperation. "Will you shut up? Why are you trying to make this into an argument?"

"I'm not." I throw the stone toward the water and hear an unsatisfying *thud* as it hits the ground.

"You are! There's been some underlying resentment on your part for a long time, and I have no idea what I've done to cause it."

"Underlying resentment? Seriously? Why would I have any reason to resent you?"

"That's the question of the day, isn't it?"

"How could you even ask that? I tell you everything. You know me probably better than I know myself, and—"

"And that's exactly how I know you've been harboring something—for years."

There's hurt there. I can hear it, and I wonder if it's a reflection of what's in my eyes because that's how I feel sometimes when I look at her. It's not an overt betrayal I feel, but yes . . . I feel betrayed.

"Eve, talk to me. You can tell me anything."

I take a moment to gather my thoughts and grasp upon a memory. I'm not quite sure how to word it all yet, but I let the memory take me where it may. "You know how when we were little, we would blindfold ourselves and take turns leading each other around the yard?"

Lyn smiles. "Sometimes we wouldn't even say anything. We'd just know because we could feel each other."

"Exactly! That took a lot of trust, and I've always trusted you, but after your accident . . ."

"That happened over ten years ago!"

"I know. I just . . ." I shake my head, at a loss for what to say next.

"Eve, what happened was not your fault. You know that, right? I think deep down, you do. You couldn't have done anything—"

"I know, I just . . ."

Lyn nods.

"I don't trust myself to live without limits the way you do—the way I used to," I begin. I don't know where the words are coming from, but they've found their voice, and I'm not going to stop. "And it pisses me off. I look at you and see you doing amazing things, and I'm so proud of you— so proud—but I'm scared to death too. If that never happened, would I be the same way you are, the way I was? Would I be free?"

"Oh, Eve." Lyn wraps her arms around me, but it does nothing to comfort me. I might have given my feelings a voice, but they still haven't been assuaged. I still feel trapped.

"You know I never blamed you, right? You said you didn't want to go, and I'm stubborn. I decided to go anyway. All I could imagine were your pointy elbows landing on my stomach." Lyn leans over and demonstrates, and I laugh, loving and hating the way she can make light of the situation.

"Yeah, but you just kept going, even after months of being in a cast, and all the physical therapy and knowing you'd never be able to dance again . . ."

Lyn sighs. "That's all true, but look at what it has opened up for me. Had I pursued dance, I never would have discovered some of the passions I have now. All those months cooped up, I was able to do a lot of internet searches and reading. What's that saying? When one door closes, blah, blah, blah."

I give her a small smile. "Yeah, I guess. I just wish I could find the door or an open window or something."

"Don't take it out on yourself. Seriously. Move on. I have."

We sit in silence for a few minutes, the sound of the waves lulling us into a peaceful relaxation.

"I think I hit my head," I say. I watch the water, waiting for the moment when it almost feels as if I'm above it, flying.

"Huh?" Lyn's kicking her foot out in front of her, disturbing rocks and grass, and I stop watching the water to watch her instead.

"That's gotta be the only explanation, right? Maybe we both hit our heads?"

We sit for a couple of minutes staring out at the lake, and I can feel tension creeping back into my shoulders and neck. Lyn breaks the silence. "Nah, you've always been like that . . ."

It takes me a minute to remember what she's referring to, and when I do, I hit her. Her shoulders are shaking with silent laughter, but she sticks her tongue out at me anyway.

I lean toward her. "Is that an invitation?" I ask while wriggling my brows suggestively.

"Ewww!" Lyn shrieks. "Eve, that's disgusting!" But we're both laughing out loud at this point, and the tension is broken once again.

"But you offered!" I say. I swipe a tear from my eye as my laughter slows and Lyn dabs at hers with her fingers.

"I think you'll remember," Lynn says finally.

"You already do?"

"Maybe," she says. I can feel her watching me, but I don't turn because if I do, she'll tell me her thoughts, and right now, it's just another mystery I get to play with, so I don't want to remember. Not yet. She knows that too.

Lyn kicks her foot out in front of her again, shrugs, and changes the subject. "That was gross, Eve."

I snicker. "Then my job here is done."

## Chapter 9

I'd wanted to tell Lyn about Nick's brother. I'd wanted to tell her how my heart seemed to stop when I saw him, how I actually held my breath, but I hadn't. At least, I don't think I did. I can't remember. I can't remember a lot of things after my conversation with Lyn, like getting to my room or going through my nightly routine of washing my face and brushing my teeth. But I do remember not being able to sleep. My eyes didn't want to close, so I lay there, my eyes glued to the ceiling I could hardly see in the waning light coming from the window, and in the silence, I thought about the oddities of the house.

In the silence that isn't silence. And that's another thing: there's an underlying noise, a pulse, a vibration. It has been there since the beginning, but it's one of those distractions people don't think about when other things are going on. I can only liken it to the sound of my own heart beating in my ears when everything is quiet or if I've overexerted myself. It's not the steady beat one would hear when listening through a stethoscope—or when reflecting, in silence, upon one's own heart. It's . . . off. And the sound isn't in my ears; it's everywhere. So, as I thought about the oddities of the house, this was another peculiarity I added to the growing list.

Since I couldn't sleep, I was tempted to get back up and wander the halls to see what else I could discover. Even though I don't feel anything threatening within the walls of the manor, there's also something eldritch about it too. More than just the dark and dusty rooms I've encountered and miles of corridors, it's as if the house is a living entity itself, and I must tiptoe lest I disturb its repose.

It's funny how the mind works. My fear of water, lack of sleep, the unquiet silence, and thoughts of the slumbering house coalesced in my mind and soon I had myself believing that I as well as the house had been swallowed whole by a huge watery monster bent on my demise. It seems foolish now, in the light of day, but it all seemed so much clearer to me last night, and the thought made me want to stick to the four walls around me.

I was relieved when a sound of another sort outside my door had me propping myself up on my elbows. I thought maybe it was Lyn trying to find my room, and with the number of rooms on the floor, I wouldn't have been surprised she had trouble finding mine. I switched on the small lamp by my bed and rose to let her in. After the afternoon's conversation, I was feeling particularly close to her and thought a little company would be nice.

I was about to open the door when I heard a heated, yet whispered discussion. The sibilants hissed, and some of the words were whispered with insistency—but I couldn't hear any distinct words. *What if she's out there?* The thought of Lyn being chastised had me seeing red.

With my eyes already narrowed into a glare, I yanked the door open, prepared to unleash my wrath, when I saw Hammond and Gail. Their equal scowls descended upon me, and the intensity in their eyes raised goosebumps on my skin. I quickly scanned the hallway—Lyn was nowhere around— then opened my mouth to say something to make the whole encounter a little less awkward, but the shadows behind them seemed to grow, making their presence and their glowers even more intimidating. Gone, it seemed, were the formal yet accommodating and kind caretakers of the estate. In their place stood two apparent imposters. Instead of speaking, I took a step back, closed my mouth, closed the door—making sure to lock it—and leaned my back against its solid mass.

*What the hell was that?* I sank to the floor, not quite ready to stop acting as an additional barrier in case they tried to come in, and thought about their whispered words and the menacing look in their eyes. I couldn't decide if I felt the threat was toward one of them or me, and I cocked my head, pressing my ear against the door, hoping to hear something that would give me a clue.

It wasn't long though before I heard their feet shuffle away from the door. I waited a few minutes, got up, opened the door a crack to see if they were in the hallway, and when I noticed they were no longer there, that's when I felt comfortable enough to make my way back to the bed.

And now, in late morning as I sit at the kitchen table, I feel even less motivated to do anything. I'm ready to go back to bed, but I know I should stay up or I'll ruin my whole sleep pattern when I go back to work.

My heart starts hammering in my chest at the thought, and I cover my mouth as nausea courses through me. I can feel the muscles in my shoulders bunching, and my eyes dart back and forth like I'm on the lookout for danger. *Again? Why?* I'm not thinking of water, I'm thinking of my job.

Curiouser and curiouser.

I've always liked my job. At least, I thought I did. My heart drops again when I realize I can't remember what I do. But I knew before! *What is going on with me? Does my job have something to do with how I got here?* I don't think it's possible, but right now it's the only explanation I can come up with. Tears don't just threaten; they burst through and race down my cheeks. And I let them come. Yes, I'm feeling sorry for myself. But I don't care. I don't know what's happening, and it's scary as hell. And yeah, there's Lyn. I can talk to her, I know, but she's not exactly sharing information with me either. There's something she's hiding, something about how we got here, and although I don't want to push her—at least the part of me that doesn't want to know—I can't help but feel she has an obligation to fill me in.

I wipe my hand across my eyes and sniffle. Crying isn't going to do anything. It's not going to solve any problems. I need to talk to a doctor. I need a PET scan or a CT scan or a psychologist to tell me what's wrong with me.

No.

Before we leave, if I haven't figured it out, I need to talk to Lyn. I nod and wipe my eyes again before taking the napkin in front of me and blowing my nose. Resolved, I take a deep breath and let it out slowly. Sometimes, a good cry is all that's needed, and sometimes focusing on something else helps one find clarity where it's needed most. This manor will definitely do nicely as a focus. And nothing needs to get solved today. That's enough to center me.

A mug of hot tea sits before me, and I take a sip, allowing it to move the lump in my throat down a fraction or two. The manor is quiet, relaxing, and I take another deep breath. It *is* peaceful here, calming in a way I can't fully comprehend or explain. My eyes close and I allow myself to be in the moment, to completely immerse myself in the solitude. Once the retreat is over, I'll make an appointment to see what's going on if it's needed. Until then, I might as well enjoy what I can here.

I try to focus on the silence, but there's so much going on in my head, I can't think straight. I don't allow myself to think of going to a doctor, and unable to dwell on that, my mind refuses to settle on a specific topic, instead jumping from how I got here and the massive amounts of water around the island to the woman Lyn calls a ghost, then to Nick and his brother and back to all the water. I sigh in frustration.

Raising my arms in a stretch, I get up and dump the rest of the tea down the sink, rinse out the mug and put it in the dishwasher, and walk out of the kitchen. I have nowhere in particular I need to be, and although that suits me just fine, I can't help feeling a little restless. Am I actually missing the hustle and bustle of the everyday? How funny.

I used to have a dog named Pepper. He was a miniature schnauzer my parents bought. I don't know why I'm thinking about him, except for the fact that he would follow me around the house, especially when I was on edge. Like now. It's like I'm waiting for the other shoe to drop, and I have no idea when that will be. Pepper would block my path and put up a paw, or he'd keel over and play dead until I rubbed his belly. Anything to get me to pay attention to him, and I'd forget my restlessness or push it aside. He was good at that.

But he's not here.

I have no idea where Hammond and Gail are, but I don't feel a need to find them. They're probably busy and don't need me asking questions they don't likely have the answers to anyway. That's what I tell myself, at least.

For some reason, I'm content to sit back and let this all play out. Despite the fact I should be looking for answers. *Why the hell am I not looking for answers?*

I walk past the living room and through hallways, passing open doors leading to rooms I've yet to explore and passing closed doors that dissuade me from entering. Whereas normally I would jump at the chance to snoop, I don't feel up to it. I'm too on edge.

I walk around the library again, and I take a peek out the window. A small but overgrown garden sits only meters away.

Purple flowers interspersed with dandelions and daisies fight for territory alongside uncut grass and weeds. It's exactly what I need. More so, I need the fresh air that comes with being outdoors.

And suddenly, I can't breathe. My heart feels like lead in my chest and my stomach undulates like when I'm on a rollercoaster. Every muscle is tensed to act, and anxiety rolls through me. The manor is nowhere near small, but looking outside has instigated an overwhelming bout of claustrophobia. The walls feel as if they're closing in on me. Even the ceiling is getting lower. I pull at my shirt, feeling it's too close to my skin. *Air. I need air!*

There's a door near the window, and I sprint toward it, anticipating a soft breeze and the smell of wildflowers even with the lake so close by. Finally reaching the door, I fumble at the lock, desperation coursing through me with my unexplainable need to feel the air and take in full, deep breaths of it.

With the door open, my eyes close and I draw a deep breath. Then another. I'm halfway down the stairs when I cut my inhale short, the view filtering through striking me as odd. *How the hell did I get on the front porch?* Confused, I finish my descent and look up at the house dumbly. Turning slowly, I take in the lake, the dock, and the house once again. How did

I get to the front of the house? I climb the stairs two at a time and open the front door. It leads to the foyer, just like it has every time I've stepped through the door before. So, how did I get here from the library in the back of the house?

Frowning, I open and close the door several times, expecting the view to miraculously change.

It doesn't. My heart starts racing, but it's a mixture of excitement and fear. I feel as if I've just come off one of those rides that plunges from an extraordinary height, but tenfold. This is beyond anything that has ever happened to me before, and a smile lifts the corners of my mouth before turning into a full-on grin. That. Was. So. Cool! This is the sort of stuff I've been searching for. The bizarre and supposedly impossible . . . I want it to happen again.

Abandoning the front door, I walk through the rooms until I come to the side door in the library once more. I look out. Down a few concrete steps, the small garden mocks me, its tall weeds and straggly flowers bobbing in the breeze. The yard, sparsely covered in grass and weeds, gently slopes down to the lake beyond. I hadn't been paying attention to what was beyond the first time, but this time, I notice the rocks, made dark with the falling shadows of a new storm hovering just off to the east, that line the shore and a tree limb, skeletal and reaching, that must have come in on the current.

Taking a deep breath, I open the door and step outside, half expecting, and hoping, to be on the front porch once again.

My feet land on the concrete steps. Four down, and I'm on the ground. I look up at the house and then down to the rocky shore. I'm tempted to try it again and am about to run up the steps when Gail appears in the doorway.

Startled, I jump back and muffle a scream. "Whoa! You scared me!"

"Oh! I'm so sorry, Eve. I didn't mean to frighten you. I saw you and wondered if you needed anything is all." The Gail I see standing before me is a far cry from the menacing one I saw in the hall outside my door last night. Her eyes are filled only with concern and warmth.

"No, it's my fault, but listen, it's the weirdest thing," I say before telling her about my teleportation from here to the front porch.

"Are you sure you're feeling all right?" Gail stares down at me from the house, her eyes shadowed by the small overhang above the door.

"I know it doesn't sound possible, but I swear it just happened," I insist. "I stepped out the doorway you're standing in right now, only I landed on the front porch. How does that happen?"

"Well, that certainly is strange," she mutters as she fumbles with something just inside the doorway and out of my view. "So, did you need anything?" she asks absently.

"No, but did you hear what I said?"

"You're here to relax, my dear. What it sounds like to me is that you meant to go out the side door, got distracted, and went out the front door, thinking you went out the side door instead. It sounds like you're still overtaxing yourself. Relax. Just relax. You don't need anything?"

"No," I insist as I consider her words. I *was* thinking of going through the house and out the front door. Is it possible I did exactly that? With the way things have been going, it's not out of the realm of possibility . . . but still, I went out the side door. I *know* I did.

"Gail, are you telling me that nothing strange has ever happened here? That you've never seen anything out of the ordinary since you started working here?

"That's ridiculous. I've never encountered such a thing. I—"

"But have others told you about anything strange here?"

"I-I . . ." Gail starts wringing her hands again.

"Gail, listen. I'm telling the truth. I walked out *this* door—this one right here—and landed on the *front* porch!" My voice is raised, and I can feel myself shaking with excitement—and maybe just a bit of hysteria. I want her confirmation. I want to experience more, so I have even more proof. My eyes dart every which way, my mind already on where I should explore next.

"Fine then, that's just fine." Gail's words show she's not listening to a thing I've said. She's humoring me. Her brows are creased in concern, but she's muttering to herself again, and I don't know if her concern is for me or for whatever it is she's distracted about to begin with. Suddenly, the scowl from last night appears, and without another word, she turns around and disappears from view.

My eyebrows knit together. *I'm on a retreat in the* Twilight Zone. But then, I've always liked that show. I smile. I've yet to explore the house, and what could possibly have happened to put me on the porch has me pumped to see what else the house is hiding. Following Gail, I decide to further investigate.

## Chapter 10

The house is a maze of hallways with closed and opened doors, each containing a secret to unravel. I wonder if I'll have enough time to nose through everything thoroughly before it's time to leave. Somehow, I doubt it.

Although the house is bright and cheerful in some rooms, others are cold and dark, as if Gail and Hammond, and the rest of the world, have forgotten them. One set of doors opens to a massive dining room. The air is damp, and cold light enters from dingy windows with discolored, gathered empire balloon shades hanging limply with grime and mold from rods placed along the tops. A long, sturdy wooden table for twelve sits in the center of the room. What used to be a white tablecloth runner, now yellowing from time, lines the middle of the table and drapes several inches off the far sides. I step up to one of the renaissance brocade chairs that are pushed in and waiting for diners to take their seats. I dare not sit though, and fear that just a touch will be enough to make the chair collapse. Everything in the room has the appearance of being too brittle, too fragile.

Cobwebs and dust blanket everything, the table, chairs, the floor, and I can almost hear the faint whispers of memories floating through the room—an echoing laugh here, a loud voice over there. I spin slowly, imagining what the room must have looked like once, and startle when I see Hammond standing by the doors. He's so silent, I can almost imagine he's part of the illusion of this room, a ghost lost to the shadows of time.

"Hammond?"

"This room has not been used for a long while," he tsks while his eyes roam over the windows and numerous dust motes. He looks at me solemnly before turning in the doorway and leaving as quietly as he came in.

I spin slowly once more, pondering why this room has been abandoned when I spy a closed door on the opposite side of the room. I amble toward it. Hammond said something about some rooms needing to be closed off at times, so there's the possibility it's locked anyway. Then again, maybe not.

The doorknob turns in my hand, and I'm just starting to get excited when I pull, and nothing happens. I mutter my discontent and pull once more for good measure, fully expecting the same resistance, when the door opens. I have to catch myself from stumbling backward.

Glancing behind me to see if Gail or Hammond is there, I quickly move through the door when I see no one and shut it behind me.

It appears as though I'm in another part of the house entirely, and my eyes scan everything quickly before I step further in. I'm in a large dark hallway lit only by dim standing lamps interspersed. I can see doors on either side, but because the hallway is so wide, it's decorated in much the same way as a room would be. There are tables with knickknacks and chairs situated in nooks. Shelves with books and photographs line the walls.

This part of the house looks older, older than the dining room even. Not only is it not as bright and airy as some other parts of the house, but the smell of mildew is more distinct. The paint on the walls looks dingy and is chipped in a few places, and cracks, some larger than others, run down the length of some of the walls, fanning out like spider veins. A runner down the length of the hall looks old and worn, fraying at the edges. Even the furniture, the couches and chairs tucked away, is shabbier here. Their colors are faded with time and stained with watermarks.

Moving into an alcove, I glance at some of the bindings of the books on a shelf and am happy to recognize many of the titles. I pull out *Tuesdays with Morrie*, one I've been meaning to read, but the binding starts to crumble. I yank my fingers away and wonder if all the volumes here are so fragile. It's not as if this one is so old. I lean in to get a closer look at the titles when I hear a noise behind me. Thinking it's Gail or Hammond coming to tell me something more about the manor, I summon a polite smile and turn to greet them.

But it's not Gail or Hammond.

It's Nick's brother.

## Chapter 11

"**O**h! I'm so sorry! I thought you were someone else." I take a step back unsteadily and feel myself falling back, ready to collide with the bookshelf.

"Whoa, didn't mean to sneak up on you!" Seeing my arms windmill, he clasps my shoulders to hold me steady. "I thought you heard me coming."

I grab onto his hands on my shoulders, and after a moment, we're both still.

"I'm Ari," he says, taking his hands off my shoulders slowly as if I'm going to start flailing the moment he does.

"Eve."

"It's nice to meet you, Eve." His voice is warm and inviting, deep and a little husky. I'd wrap his voice around me if I could and burrow deep. Eyes, a piercing deep blue reminding me more of crisp winter days than of the ocean, bite into me with the same penetrating intensity as the last time I saw him. Reflexively, I hug myself.

"And you."

We stand awkwardly in the hallway for a few moments, and I feel like I do when someone scratches a chalkboard, only there's no sound. Internally, I cringe as I wait for the feeling to pass and move to walk around him. He brushes his fingers down my arm, and a shiver rises, leaving goosebumps in its wake.

"Wait." Ari pauses like he's not sure what to say. "You don't like boats?"

"What?" Of all the things he could say, this is unexpected.

"You didn't go out on the boat yesterday afternoon." He shrugs, and I hide a smile. In my head, I'm jumping up and down, giddy with the knowledge that this gorgeous man is detaining me to ask irrelevant questions while my body squirms, wishing to get away from the silent scraping of invisible fingernails.

"Oh. Uh, no. Not really," I say, unwilling to share more, and because I can't think of anything else to say without sounding like a bumbling idiot, I attempt to walk around him again.

"You know," he says, his voice stopping me in my tracks. I turn to him. "I'm terrible at flirting. How about you try to pick me up instead?"

I snort. When I glance at his face, I can see his eyes sparkling with humor, their uneasy intensity gone. It relaxes me, and my inner fidgeting calms. "Was that a line? That was the cheesiest line ever!"

"You have a better one?" He crosses his arms over his chest, his posture mirroring my own, and I'm offered a wonderful view of his biceps through the long-sleeved T-shirt hugging his torso. The dim lights can't hide them, for which I'm grateful.

It doesn't take me long to think of a reply. "I'm sorry we collided. Trust me, I'm not drunk; I'm just intoxicated by you."

"Oh-ho! Not bad! Not bad at all. How about this—do you happen to have a Band-Aid? Because I just scraped my knees falling for you."

I roll my eyes. "I've heard better," I say, taking in his warm smile and returning it with one of my own. "You know, I'd love to continue this fun exchange, but I think I need CPR instead because your last remark just took my breath away."

"I'd be happy to oblige," he says without missing a beat, and he steps toward me.

My heart beats faster and for a moment I'm filled with panic. I take a step back and one of the shelves from the bookcase digs into my shoulder. "Unfortunately for you, it was just a line."

"Ooo, she shoots, she scores." Ari's eyes are trained on me, and instead of feeling uncomfortable, I now feel powerful. "Beautiful *and* witty," he breathes.

Shifting uneasily, my hair falls in my face, but I don't tuck it back. I'm not used to compliments like that, and my face is flaming.

"Well," he says reluctantly, "I would love to stay and talk to you, but I do have business to attend to."

I smile, both relieved and disappointed. He's the one who starts to walk away this time when I ask, "You're Nick's brother, aren't you? You sound like him. He says the same thing."

Ari looks surprised. "Nick spoke of me?"

I nod. He doesn't have to know it was nothing good.

He blinks rapidly a few times, perplexed, and I'm offered a small glimpse of vulnerability. "Well, we both work for the family business. I guess some expressions are bound to rub off."

"What is it you both do?" It's none of my business, but I'm curious. Nick mentioned several houses, and I'm wondering if my guess is correct. "I'm thinking real estate."

Ari's face goes blank except for his eyes. They convey too much for me to comprehend, and again I want to shield myself from him, turn around and walk away quickly—no, run—but I'm rooted to the spot as if he's a celebrity and I'm some starry-eyed fangirl waiting for recognition.

"Nick works on Systems Maintenance, and I work on Project Completion," he finally says.

"He said something about maintaining houses earlier," I say. "Sounds like you're the guy who sells them."

"Something like that."

"Wait, does that mean Lakeview Manor is being sold?" I can't keep the disappointment out of my voice. I don't even know why I'm so upset. "I can't imagine why anyone would want to sell it."

Ari clears his throat. "It's more like the owner is thinking about closing the house down."

"What? No!" I glance around me at the warped wooden floorboards and peeling paint, but my thoughts go to the clean lines and elegance of other parts of the house. "Oh, that's too bad. I hope whoever it is has a change of heart and decides to keep it."

"Yeah, well . . ." Ari gives me a tight smile. "Sometimes we're not given a choice, you know?" He inhales deeply and smiles again. "Anyway, I better get some work done, but, um, if you're not busy later, maybe you'd like to meet up in the kitchen for something to eat?"

He lowers his head, and I can't help noticing how a lock of his dark hair falls over his forehead. It's at about the same time that my stomach drops. The thought of food—or having it with him—repulses me. "I'm sorry. I already have plans." I don't, but I can't keep my stomach from roiling at the thought of eating with him.

"With Nick?"

I keep silent. I remember I'm supposed to go out with Nick tomorrow though, and the churning subsides.

Ari shakes his head. "Sorry, that wasn't fair of me. And I get it. Heck, I'd probably go out with Nick too if we weren't such opposites." He grins. "It would help if we weren't related too, and if he wasn't such an ass."

I chuckle. "I have a feeling he'd say the same about you." I turn to leave. "Bye, Ari."

"Hey, wait! You think I'm going to give up that easily?" Ari touches my arm and a delicious chill travels through me, simultaneously as the hairs on the back of my neck rise. He steps closer, our faces inches apart. "Are you busy tomorrow night?"

My breath hitches as he stares into my eyes, and I hesitate. I'm undeniably drawn to this man, and despite Nick assuring us Ari isn't dangerous, my instinct is screaming for me to run away. So why can't I?

"I—I'm . . ." Licking my lips, I step back only to find Ari leaning in, his eyes traveling from my mouth to my eyes and back again.

"I'm not going to coerce you. You can say no if you want." Ari smiles and touches my cheek. "But that will mean I'll have to ask you again." He steps back and leans against the opposite wall. "You'll break down and say yes, eventually. I mean, how could you continue to say no to this?" He gives me the saddest puppy-dog-eyes look ever, and I laugh.

"Yeah, that would get to me sooner or later." I give him a once over. He hasn't done anything that would make me think his intentions are bad or said anything I've needed to question, but my instincts still tell me saying yes isn't a good idea. That there's something I should guard myself against.

I shake my head, but try to remain friendly, "I'm sorry. Maybe another time."

Ari gives me another breathtaking smile that makes me want to take back my words, then steps away from the wall. He begins walking backward down the hall, keeping his attention on me. "I *will* ask you again."

I smile. "Bye, Ari."

And then I'm left staring at the corner he has disappeared around. A shiver runs through me and I tell myself it's a draft even though the air remains stagnant and close. In some ways, I want to go after him, tell him I've changed my mind, but in others, I feel like I've dodged a bullet. There's something about him I can't put my finger on. He's like the water: beautiful to look at, but I don't want to get too close. I sigh.

Ready to burst with everything I need to tell Lyn, I abandon my explorations and head back to the dining room. It's the only way I know to get back to the part of the house I'm familiar with. However, when I open the door, it's not the dining room I find; it's the library, the room with the door that should have led me to the side of the house but took me instead to the front porch.

For just a moment, ice courses through my veins. It's not possible, yet it has happened. Again.

I have to find Lyn.

## Chapter 12

**I** race upstairs only to realize I have no idea where Lyn's room is. Once I get to mine, I shout her name and wait a few moments. When she doesn't respond, I race back down the stairs, looking through the living room and some of the other rooms before I make my way to the kitchen.

It's not there. Instead, I've come upon a dead end.

Retracing my steps to the living room, I once again make my way to the kitchen. It's possible that in my excitement, I took a wrong turn, but when I encounter the dead end for a second time, I know I'm experiencing what is now becoming a normal occurrence.

I see Gail carrying a pail of water and rush up to her. "Gail, have you seen Lyn? Or the kitchen?"

She squints her eyes at me in confusion. "The kitchen? The kitchen's where it has always been, dear, down the hall, first door to the left." She points, and I feel a bit sheepish. Maybe the kitchen *has* been there the whole time. *But that can't be.*

I feel as if I'm about to run into a white rabbit I'll have to chase down a hole. Telling Lyn will lead her to come up with all sorts of bizarre theories about the house itself and the land it sits on. And that's what I want. I want someone to come up with weird scenarios because if there is a remote chance that any one of them could be true, then it means it's not all in my mind, and I'm not going crazy thinking things that aren't possible. I'm already forgetting stuff and seeing people others haven't seen. Nosing through rooms that move of their own accord is not something else I want to have to worry about.

There's a theory that your mind tries to help you figure things out. At least, I'm pretty sure I've heard this somewhere. Dreams are supposed to help a person figure out what's going on in their waking life, and I'm sure there has to be something similar when one is already awake too. What if all this forgetting is protecting me from something really horrible, like Lyn said? Maybe the porch incident is part of it all. Maybe my brain just can't cope with whatever it is that happened.

Slowing my steps, I continue down the hall, all the while assessing myself. Physically, I feel fine. A bit tired. I woke up a little achy, but I'm fine. So, that leaves mentally. Did I see something I shouldn't have? Learn some truth that's too much for me? I automatically think of my parents. I would know if something had happened to them. I would feel it. I know I would.

I look through the threshold Gail pointed out, and sure enough, it's the kitchen. Even better, Lyn's sitting at the table, a mug of tea in front of her. I open my mouth to say something, but I don't even know where to start. Luckily, it doesn't matter because the moment Lyn sees me, she rises from the table, her tea sloshing dangerously close to the rim of the mug. "You have found yourself a doozy this time, Eve," she says, her eyes bright.

"What are you talking about?"

"This house! Have you walked around?" she asks. She's practically bouncing on the balls of her feet, so I know whatever has happened to her, it has to have been pretty big.

"What happened to you?" I ask, relieved I'm not the only one and anxious to hear if Lyn's experiences match mine.

"So, something has happened to you too?" Lyn jumps in the air and grasps my shoulders. "Whew! We're in a haunted house! A truly haunted house!"

I jump up and down with her for a few seconds. "Lyn, just tell me already! What happened?"

Lyn pulls me over to the table where we both sit, and she tells me about some of the rooms she's been in. "It's like the walls breathe," she says, and I'm reminded of my feelings last night of the house sleeping. "There are shadows and when I turn around to look, they're not there, and then, I came upon this one room that looked like an old, unused gym, and I wasn't really interested in that, but when I turned around to walk out the *same* door I went in, I was in a completely different part of the house!"

My eyes widen. "That's exactly what happened to me!" I tell her about my adventures with the side door in the library and the dining room and also tell her my thoughts from last night about feeling like the house was sleeping and about the weird, underlying sound that permeates the house.

Lyn is silent, listening. Her eyes widen and she nods. "I hear it." She listens for a few moments more, her gaze focusing on something I can't see. "You said you heard about this house before," she says, her voice as distant as her gaze. "You never heard it was haunted?" Lyn takes a sip of her tea.

"No! As I said, I've heard of this place, but no one seems to know anything about it."

Lyn's eyes focus on me. "And now we do," she says with a smile.

"And now we do," I repeat.

"So, what's next?" Her eyes narrow in question.

I'm planning to explore more, but there's something else she's thinking about. "What do you mean?"

"Come on, Eve. Do you remember how you got here yet?"

I blink. I haven't even been thinking about it. I haven't been thinking about the water either. The last couple of hours have been fabulous in that sense. Wandering the halls of the house and learning more about its mysteries has calmed me like nothing else so far. I've felt no anxiety at all, but the mere mention of *how* brings all my unease back. "No."

Lyn looks down at the table in disappointment.

"Why does it matter to you so much, and why won't you tell me what you remember?"

"The last time, the doctors said it was best to let you remember on your own. They said it was important not to push you, remember?" And the thing is, I do remember them saying that. Something about not wanting to create false beliefs and how everyone has their own reality and must remember the reality they own. "And I thought that maybe if you remember, then you'd want to leave a bit sooner."

I shake my head in disbelief. "You just said how cool it is this house is haunted! Don't you want to explore more? Why do you want to leave?"

117

That faraway look comes back into her eyes, almost as if she's in a trance, but as she speaks, her eyes focus again. "It's just so lonely here, isn't it? It's eerie. It's like everything is waiting for something . . . and I guess I'm missing being home."

I understand what she's saying. It *is* lonely, quiet, even with the others here. It's eerie too, but in such a way that I feel no fear. Lyn says she's missing home, but I feel like I've arrived. I stand up and lean over Lyn, hugging her. "You can leave if you want, Lyn, but there are only five days left. I want to stay."

I leave the kitchen and am happy when things stay the way I'm used to so I can make my way to the front door. A bit of fresh air would be nice after so many closed rooms.

Although the sky has darkened significantly, the sun still provides enough light in reds, pinks, and yellows. The air is warm, and I need the exercise and time away from . . . I don't know. There are too many things I don't want to think about, some bigger than others, and I always try to distract myself when there's something I don't want to deal with, like the time I made out with Danny Johnson because I didn't want to face the fact that my dog of twelve years, Pepper, had just been put to sleep, or the time I got shitfaced because I didn't want to face the fact that I didn't get into the university I wanted. Then there's Lyn's accident . . . I grappled with the reality of that one for a day, not wanting to face it . . . But for the first time in my life, whatever it is I don't want to face has to be pretty major for me to not even have an inkling of what it is. *What the hell did I screw up?*

As I make my way around the back of the house, my mind whirls with everything that's happened in the last two days.

When I reach the corner of the house, I can either turn and continue alongside it toward the front or head off deeper onto the property. I choose the latter. I'm on a small island, so I'm certainly not going to get lost. The possibility of it being big enough that I don't immediately see water would be a relief too.

Aquaphobia is embarrassing. The anxiety created is almost unbearable. My heart quickens, I begin to sweat, but when I'm going through it, the embarrassment isn't the worst part. It's the thought that if I get any closer, something terrible will happen—I'll die a horrible death. Some horrid water creature—a shark or giant squid or some icky thing with razor-sharp teeth that hasn't even been identified yet—will drag me down into the murky depths, and as I gurgle my last breaths, my blood will mix with the water surrounding me, turning it crimson red . . .

Yeah, pleasant thoughts like that.

I haven't even gone thirty steps when I trip over something hiding in the undergrowth. Two steps more and I trip again, barely catching myself before landing face first. The trees here are denser, and their roots, hiding beneath overgrown wisps of grass, stick up through the ground haphazardly. Rocks big and small practically stand in line waiting to trip me up. I look back at the house and sigh.

Before I even lift my foot, something in my periphery catches my attention. In the distance, and walking parallel to me, someone is heading toward the front of the house. It looks like Lyn, and I call out to her, but then I remember I just left Lyn in the kitchen. She continues walking, but I hesitate. It's not Lyn's gait. It's the woman—my ghost, as Lyn would say. No one has mentioned anyone else living on the island, not Gail or Hammond and not Nick or Ari. I think back to my encounter with her in the hall, how uneasy she made me, how she disappeared around the corner without Hammond seeing her. Perhaps she is a ghost. I hasten a slow jog in her direction, careful to lift my feet, before coming to a halt.

Right in front of me, there's a small footbridge. The water underneath gurgles softly as it meanders over small rocks and pebbles, making its way farther off to nourish plants or become rakish and suitable only for mosquitoes. I have no clue. *Of course, there has to be a bridge. Of course, there has to be water.*

My heart beats sporadically. I could go back the way I came and lose time, or I could suck it up and cross the bridge. It wouldn't be more than four steps before I was on the other side, and the water itself isn't deep. The bridge looks to be more for appearances than for necessity, and I could probably just jump over the small creek, but I'm too scared.

Trembling, my breath already ragged before I've even taken a step, I tentatively lift my right foot off the ground only to return it seconds later. Sweat courses down my back and the palms of my hands; I take a deep breath, then another. I'm psyching myself up because I can *do* this! My leg shakes as I raise it once more, and I roar with frustration as it comes back down no closer to the wooden slats. I can't do this. A tear slowly makes a track down my cheek and I angrily brush it away as I turn, my head hanging in shame as I head in the direction from which I came.

The woman, at least from this distance, looks so much like Lyn—like me—from the length of her wavy brown hair to her build. I can't see her features though; she's too far away. She must have stopped to view my struggle because she's still there when I turn back to look.

She's obviously curious about me too. But then she starts walking again. Why doesn't she wait? Why doesn't she come over? Taking a deep breath, I force myself over the bridge, my curiosity, for once, greater than my fear. My heart is pumping as if it'll explode as I run across without looking down. Stopping only when I feel the grass beneath my feet once again, I bend over and put trembling hands on my knees. My breaths are short and quick, and I turn around slowly, afraid this too is just a figment of my imagination and I'll still be on the wrong side of the bridge. But no. I did it.

I did it!

I jump into the air excitedly, fist-bumping the sky. I've forgotten the woman—I'm all about my own achievement. I'm invincible. I am a legend. I am a fucking god.

Facing the bridge, I look at it pointedly and give it the finger.

Tempted to cross it again because I can, my adrenaline-weakened legs say to call it a day. I smile and obey. After all, I faced a fear today—and conquered the shit out of it! Instead, I pivot to face the house. The view is breathtaking. From this side, I notice the small rise the manor sits on. The sun, mostly hiding its brilliance under the horizon, continues to light the sky in all sorts of pinks, yellows, oranges, and reds. The house, standing at the center of this explosion of color, almost looks as if it is the object that exploded.

I challenge my eyes to see something drab and uninspired. The skies, the water, and the house are all off-limits, it appears, until the slightest movement catches my eye, and I focus on a small casement on the first floor of the manor. Someone's there. It's the woman—or ghost—and I can swear she's looking at me, her eyes boring into mine even though I know it's too far for me to tell for sure. A shiver passes through me, raising the hairs on the back of my neck.

There's no way she could have made it there so quickly.

My head swivels to the now empty space she occupied on the land outside before spinning back to the casement. She's still staring, so I stare back, watching as she places her right hand upon her cheek.

➤ The House on the Lake

# Chapter 13

After an evening of searching for the woman and an even longer night of tossing and turning, I surprisingly find myself without an appetite this morning. The woman was gone when I went inside last night, of course, and I couldn't find Lyn again to tell her of the ghost or my achievement. Now, after my eyes have opened for what seems the two-hundredth time and the light streaming through the windows is enough to see by, I decide to start the day. Nick is coming to take us to lunch and seeing him is something to look forward to.

When I stumble into the kitchen, trying to rub the heaviness from my eyes, Gail is there fluttering around me, asking me what I want to eat and acting overly concerned when I tell her I will just stick with a cup of tea.

"You must eat."

"I'm not hungry," I insist. "Really, I'm fine. I'm sure I'll make up for it at lunch."

Gail reaches out to touch me as if she is about to take my temperature with the back of her hand, but stops herself and sits next to me instead. "But you didn't eat last night either," she says softly, her brows furrowed. "Are you sure I can't get you something? You have to keep up your strength."

"I'm fine, as healthy as a horse. I just have some things on my mind is all."

"Eat!" she cries angrily. Her eyes are slits, her fingers clasped together so tightly they appear bloodless. Gail clears her throat and her eyes soften. "Please," she whispers, "just one apple?"

I laugh nervously, reminded of the night both she and Hammond were so . . . animated. "Fine. If an apple will make you happy, I'll have an apple."

Gail reaches for the fruit from a basket on the counter and places it in front of me. "I should have suggested eggs and bacon then," she comments as she rises to her feet. "Enjoy your day, Eve," she says as if she never lost her composure. "And remember . . ." She closes her eyes and lifts a finger. "Relax, reflect, release."

She leaves the kitchen without another word, and after picking up and contemplating the apple for a moment, I rise to my feet and place it back in the basket. My head is too addled, my stomach too unsettled to eat.

A few hours later, and my head and stomach are still at odds. I collapse onto one of the overstuffed couches in the living room. I've now seen the entire island, and I think I've explored almost every room, even looking in the attic again. The woman is nowhere to be found, and I'm seriously considering Lyn's theory of her being a ghost. It's not as if it's a stretch to believe with the other things that have been going on.

I think it's time for me to bring Lyn in on the woman, and I get up to go talk to her. I waved to her earlier when I saw her going into the library, but Lyn has a knack for knowing when I need alone time, so after hesitating for a moment, she waved back and continued on her way.

As I walk through the living room, there are several things I never noticed before. The scent of must I've noticed in other parts of the house is now obvious here, and the tables have a thin film of dust. I run my finger across one of them, and the dust sticks together like it's mixed with a fine mist. In the corners of the ceiling, green and black mold splay in snowflake patterns. Even the metal accents around the room, like the fireplace poker and shovel and the hinges on cabinets, have touches of rust on edges and creases. Too busy marveling at the grandeur of the place, I must not have taken it in fully. No wonder Gail and Hammond are so busy. They have their work cut out for them.

On one of the tables, sits a candelabra unlike any I've ever seen. It's lit even though it's not dark in the room. I go over to peer down at it, lowering myself to view it from eye level. The base is intricately carved into the shape of a tree trunk which splits into two limbs, each dividing to form smaller branches. On each side, one of the stronger-looking branches cradles a candleholder on which sits a small, lit white candle.

I'm so absorbed by the candelabra, the sharp intake of breath behind me is startling, and I straighten. One hand knocks into the candelabra and reaching to catch it, my elbow tips a vase filled with withered flowers to the floor where it shatters.

"Look at what you're doing!" yells Gail, her face a mask of anger as she sets down another bucket of water and puts her hands on her hips.

"I'm so sorry," I say. Making sure the candelabra is safely standing on the table, I bend to pick up the dead flowers and shards of a vase that can't possibly be fixed.

"Sorry? She says she's sorry!" continues Gail. "This house needs care! Day in and day out, I do everything I can to make sure things keep running smoothly. You think it's a walk in the park? You think things just work by themselves? It's dying! And *I'm* the one pulling all the strings, *I'm* the one who's tidying up after every mess, *I'm* the one who's working nonstop so you can relax, reflect, release, aren't I? *Aren't I?*"

Slowly, I rise to my feet and take a step back, pieces of the vase in my hands. I'm so shocked by her outburst, I can barely find words to respond. "I didn't—"

"Didn't what? *Think?* Decide to make a better decision? Wonder what you could possibly—"

"Hey!" Lyn's voice is thunderous as it bounces off the walls of the room, and Gail pales as her eyes go wide. "Who the hell do you think you are, yelling like that at her? Where do you get off? Give me the number of the fucking owner now, so I can get them to fire your ass!"

Lyn storms in through the door, advancing on the caretaker as if she's going to take her out with a single blow. Gail backs away.

"Oh, Eve," Gail says, wringing her hands, suddenly timid as her gaze shifts over me. "Oh, what did I do? I'm terribly sorry. Please forgive me."

It's only then I realize what I must look like. My hands are trembling, and my knees are weak. I've never been yelled at, not like that for no apparent reason. I place fragments of the vase on the table and bend down to pick up more.

"Eve, what are you doing?" Lyn demands, her anger shifting to me. "You don't have to pick that up."

"It's ok. I knocked it over." My mind tries to process exactly what happened, and when Gail moves toward me, I flinch. She stops immediately and begins kneading her fingers once again.

"You knocked it over because she practically scared you half to death." If Lyn's eyes could shoot daggers, Gail would be on the ground with gouts of blood oozing from dozens of wounds. She continues to stride toward us both, her glare never leaving Gail for a second. "I saw the whole thing. I came in here to see if you wanted to go for a walk, and there she was, creeping up behind you, gasping like you were stealing the fucking family jewels instead of looking at a stupid candle holder."

"I-I don't know what came over me. It's just, I have so much to do, and when you—"

"Don't you *dare* try to pin this on Eve." Lyn's back is ramrod straight and her hands are on her hips. Mixed emotions flow through me. I'm proud because that's my other half, and she's sticking up for something she believes in, fighting for the underdog, even if that underdog is me. I'm mortified because I should be the one sticking up for myself, and here I am, looking like I need Lyn fighting all my battles for me. And I'm peeved because Lyn's right: where does Gail get off yelling at me when she's the one who scared me in the first place? I didn't deserve that, yet Gail looks so contrite that despite my anger, I want to forgive her.

"Gail, did you come in here to tell me something?" I ask, my voice strangely calm despite my inner turmoil.

"I—no, I was just going to check on you, and I, well, I'm just so sorry. I can't apologize enough. My yelling at you was uncalled for. It's just that so much needs to be done right now, and everything is breaking down, and—I'm so sorry."

Gail starts to back her way out of the room, her fingers still worrying each other. "Do you need anything? Can I get you anything, anything at all?" she asks as she stands in the doorway, her eyes skipping from Lyn to me and back again.

I shake my head, unable to answer her verbally, and turn away.

"Okay, then," I hear her say. Then, "And don't worry about the vase, I'll clean that up later." She stands there for half a minute; then I hear her hurry back into the room to grab the bucket, sloshing water onto the ground, before retreating with it back to the door. It seems like she has something else she wants to say, so I face her and wait, arms crossed, an eyebrow raised. Lyn continues to glare at her. At this point, the silence is so loud, I can hear my heart beating and feel its pulse in my ears. Finally, with one more apology, she leaves.

My shoulders slump and I pick up a few more pieces of glass before setting them on the table and sagging into a chair. Lyn joins me on a chair opposite me.

"That was totally uncalled for," Lyn says. Her brows are still furrowed, and her nostrils flare intermittently. "Are you okay?"

"Yeah, fine. It's just, that came out of nowhere." I think back to what I was doing and why Gail would react the way she did. She's been nothing but kind, really, albeit preoccupied, since I got here. I shake my head. I have no explanations.

"Seriously, who does she think she is and what is her game anyway? Acting all meek and wringing her hands" — Lyn fiddles with her own fingers in an exaggerated display— "and then having the audacity to yell? I don't think so. That's not okay."

We sit in silence for a few moments. My trembling subsides as I go over her tirade. *This house needs care. It's dying!* The scowls and anger I witnessed in the hall outside my door and even in the kitchen make more sense now. They were never aimed at me, and perhaps it wasn't exactly anger.

She was scared.

I lean forward, my elbows on my knees, but before I can even voice my thoughts, Lyn responds. "I don't know."

"You don't know what?"

Lyn looks at me and rolls her eyes. "I have no idea what she was talking about. It was weird. But she's friggin' crazy, so . . ."

"Lyn, you can't say that was a coincidence! We were talking about the house breathing, and now this. It's beyond just *weird*, but what the hell does it mean? There's no way the house is living."

Lyn bites the inside of her mouth while thinking. "She's definitely worried about something. She seems more and more agitated every time I see her." Lyn looks at me pointedly. "But that doesn't mean she had any right to talk to you like that," she says, "even if she has something on her mind."

"That's it?" I ask, my eyes wide. "You don't want to know what it's about?"

Lyn gives me a lopsided smile. "Don't you think you have enough going on without adding her shit into the mix?"

"I'm not talking about her shit," I insist. "I'm talking abo—" Lyn lifts her eyebrow and tilts her head. Then she crosses her arms for added measure.

"Oh fine," I sigh. "I hope you know you're ruining all my fun," I pout as I slouch back in the seat.

Lyn smiles. "Stop being a baby. So, did you want to go for a walk?"

"Huh?" Sometimes the way Lyn thinks is dizzying.

"That's why I came in here, remember?"

"Actually, I wanted to talk to you," I say. "I was going to tell you last night, but I couldn't find you. You've gotta show me the room you're staying in, by the way."

"Get on with it, Eve." She hates when I go off on tangents, so sometimes I do it on purpose. "What's up?"

"Have you seen the woman from the dock at all?"

"No, I haven't seen your ghost."

"That's the thing. I think maybe she is one."

Lyn's eyes light up and she leans forward in her chair. "Are you starting to believe?"

I smirk at her but have to admit it's sounding more and more like the only possibility. "I've seen her a couple of different times now. Three times actually." I tell Lyn about the creepy kid's bedroom and the bizarre behavior of the woman just outside the room before she disappeared around the corner. "I scared Hammond, and he almost coughed up a lung from choking on the water he was drinking. He dropped his glass too."

"Forget about Gail and Hammond! This is way more interesting. What else happened?"

"Well, a bit later, I saw her outside. I could have sworn she heard me calling to her, but when I looked up, she was gone and unless she was running at Superman speed, she made it inside the house and was looking at me from one of the windows before I had even taken ten steps." Maybe I'm exaggerating a little, but that's how it felt.

"Whoa! Eve, this is so cool! You saw a ghost!"

"Maybe." A tingle runs through me. Now that I've told Lyn, it feels real, and it even seems feasible that I've encountered something otherworldly. I decide to continue. "And then there was something really weird that happened when I was walking outside too."

"What do you mean?"

I smile, drawing it out. "There's a bridge out there, water under it and everything, and I walked over it."

"What?" Lyn exclaims. "Are you shitting me? Eve, you better not be shitting me. You walked over it?" I nod, laughing, and she pulls me up from the chair and wraps me in a hug before giving me a purposely sloppy kiss on the cheek. "That's huge, woman! Congratulations!"

"Thanks, I was pretty pleased with myself. I even gave the fucker a finger," I tell her as I swagger a little around the room.

"Woo-hoo! Go, Evie!" Lyn yells. I love that she's my cheerleader. If it's possible for my smile to widen, it does.

I exhale contentedly and fall back into a chair, kicking my legs out.

"Well, we should go outside and see if that bridge is still there, so you can give it a piece of your mind again." Lyn pretends to scowl. "Let's go show that fucker who's boss."

I laugh. "Nah, you know what? Getting yelled at tired me out. You can go pound the crap out of it if you want, but I'm going to stay right here or maybe head up to my room and take a nap."

"Fine." Lyn stands and walks toward the doorway. "Eve," she says, turning, "don't let her yelling get you down. You didn't do anything wrong."

I beam at her. "Thank you."

"I mean it," she says before continuing toward the door. "And don't forget our lunch later with Nick." She makes sure I see her wagging her eyebrows.

My exhaustion dissipates and my eyes go wide. I totally forgot about Nick!

"I knew that would get your attention." Lyn gives me a cheeky grin before sauntering out the door.

No longer tired, I sit up, my eyes returning to the candelabra, now with only one lit candle, and the broken vase and dead flowers on the table. I don't want to dwell on what happened with Gail, and that's exactly what I'll do if I stay. As Lyn said, I have enough going on right now.

➤ The House on the Lake

## Chapter 14

**I** want to try my luck with the side door once again, and I stroll through the library to get there. I sneeze. There's dust on the shelves, on the tables too. But dust doesn't accumulate that quickly. Walking over to one of the wooden side tables, I create a doodle with my index finger into the fine layer. Rubbing my finger with my thumb, I notice a greenish hue. It's not dust at all, but mold. I sneeze again. It's true the air in the house is damp with the lake surrounding it, but it wasn't like this yesterday. And if it wasn't like this yesterday, it gives even more credence to Gail's lamenting on how much she has to do.

*It's dying!*

I can't get the words out of my head, but I don't understand them. It makes me wonder how long Gail has been working at the house, if she's ever taken a few days away from it. Pity courses through me for this woman who has nothing better to do with her time than to believe the house she's working in is alive, but it doesn't add up. Not completely. There are too many strange occurrences for me to write it off as just the ramblings of an eccentric old lady, not with what I've seen and heard.

There has to be something going on. Maybe the house stands on Ley lines. Those are supposed to cause some unusual phenomena that messes with people's heads. It could even account for the ghost. Ley lines are a bit too farfetched for me though. *Ha! And ghosts aren't.* Sneezing once more, I hold my fingers to the bridge of my nose and then frown, thinking of the house moving, breathing. Lyn experienced it too. A form of mass hysteria? I don't know. It's strange and interesting and exciting and scary all at once, but I feel sad for Gail just the same, for her unshakeable devotion to what's little more than mortar and bricks, and I wonder if perhaps Lyn is right in suggesting we leave sooner.

The door to outside stands ajar, and opening it, I walk out once again, but I end up right where I am supposed to be, on the side of the house. I almost expect to see Gail when I turn to look up at the house, but she isn't there staring at me through the screen. Although I saw the two of them earlier in the kitchen, I rarely see Gail and Hammond around the house and when I do, Gail always seems to be carrying a bucket of water and Hammond is always moping, his dour appearance putting a pall on everything around. I wonder what the two of them do to keep themselves occupied.

The side door doesn't pan out the way I wanted, so I decide to check out the bridge and wonder if I'll find Lyn there too. As before, I walk to the back of the house. This time though, with purpose, I march over to where I know the small footbridge stands. It's not much to look at, really. Two parallel beams span the small creek. Nailed onto the beams are several split logs of various lengths and widths with the flattened sides up. Railings consisting of a long branch on either side of the logs are held up by smaller branches that have been nailed into the beams at the bottom. It's rudimentary construction, and I'm pretty sure I could build one myself.

Whether it's because I've conquered it before, my condescension over the bridge's appearance, or both, it's only with slight hesitation, I determinedly step over it, and once I do so, I fist bump the air before making my way across once again.

I do this three or four more times before I make myself stop right in the middle of the bridge and look down. The water babbles happily, perhaps joining in the joy of my accomplishment. I don't feel nauseated or dizzy, and I take this as a sign to explore my limitations further.

Stepping off the bridge, I take off my sandals and deliberately sink my feet into the water. It's cool and refreshing and my toes automatically curl into the rocks and pebbles beneath, their surfaces randomly covered with springy moss. A laugh bubbles up within me and I stomp my feet, splashing the water up higher and higher. It's a freedom I haven't known in I can't remember how long.

Looking up, ready to do a celebratory dance, I freeze. The "ghost" I noticed yesterday is standing where I saw her before, and she's watching me. Although too far away to discern a particular look, especially with the sun behind her throwing a shadow on her face, all I can think is that she must think I'm crazy. I lift my hands to shield my eyes from the sun, and like before, I can see her head is cocked to the side, almost as if she's studying me. Abruptly, she turns away and continues toward the front of the house.

"Wait!" I call to her as I scramble out of the water. I walk a few paces, but the dry, prickly grass, sharp rocks, and dead branches are digging into my feet. Cursing, I stumble back to my sandals and slip them on before turning again to follow the woman who, despite my call, has continued walking away from me, per usual.

"Please! Wait!" I call again, running to catch up, but by the time I reach the other side of the house, she has already disappeared around the front. Beyond irritated with my lack of progress on this particular mystery, my slow run becomes a stomp as I turn the corner. I shouldn't be surprised that she's not here, but I still look around and my eyes furrow in confusion. *Where the hell did she go?*

I stop directly in front of the house, my eyes scoping everything. The front porch is empty. No one sits on the porch swing, the chairs, or the steps leading up to the porch for that matter.

*She really is a ghost.*

My head wants to dismiss the thought, think of something more rational, but this scenario has happened far too often for me to believe it to be just a trick of the light.

My focus switches over to the dock when I hear a noise, but instead of the ghost, I see Nick tying off his boat onto one of the cleats. I didn't hear him drive in. Save for him, the dock is empty. There are no other structures I can see in which the ghost-woman would have ducked into. There is nowhere she could have gone.

Nick waves to me, and I wait for him to join me before asking questions.

"Did you see anyone when you were pulling in?"

"No, was I supposed to?

"There's Lyn, you, and me. I've met Gail, and Hammond, and Ari. Is—"

"You've met Ari?" Nick's brows furrow and he opens his mouth to say more when my glare stops him.

"Is there anyone else on the island?"

"No," Nick says, shaking his head. "Sounds like you've hit all the key players. What's this about, Eve?"

I search the immediate area again and exhale sharply. I tell Nick about the woman I saw on the dock, about how I saw her again behind the house. "Lyn says she's a ghost, and I'm starting to believe her."

"Lyn has seen her too?"

"No, that's the thing. I'm the only one, so either I'm going crazy, ghosts really do exist, or there's someone else on this island."

Nick steers me toward the porch, and we each take a seat on the steps. Nick's eyes are on the lake as he silently digests everything I've said. He's probably wondering why he invited me along to lunch, and I can't say I blame him.

"You know what?" I say, unwilling to let this bother me any longer, "just forget I said anything. I'm here on a retreat. Whoever this woman is, she hasn't tried to talk to me—if anything, she's been going out of her way to avoid me, and ghosts don't do that, right? And if it's someone else on the island, that's really something *you* need to worry about more than I do. You're the one managing this place after all. And the whole crazy bit? That's just how I roll."

Nick gives me a side-eye. "I wouldn't say you're crazy." He swivels his head, so he's looking at me directly. "A little weird, maybe . . . and you dress kind of funny."

"Shut up!" I laugh as I push him.

"And you seem to have bullying issues." He feigns a hurt expression and rubs his shoulder.

"I'm not listening to you anymore," I tell him, standing so I can go in and find Lyn.

Nick gets up too. "And you might have a hang-up that makes you walk away from the truth, but I wouldn't call you crazy."

I freeze. "What did you say?" I may not walk away from the truth, but block it out? Yeah.

Nick looks at me as if I really have gone crazy now. "What? I said you have a hang-up—"

"That makes me walk away from the truth. Why'd you say that?"

"Uh, Eve, I was just joking. I was teasing you and you were walking away."

Is that all it was? My head hangs and I shake it. "I'm sorry, Nick." I can't raise my head to look at him yet. "I swear all of this alone time is getting to me." Finally, I meet his eyes. "It's just, what you said reminded me of something. I do tend to run away from reality sometimes."

Nick strolls over to me and places his hands on my shoulders, giving them a squeeze. His gaze is filled with warmth and kindness, and I know he's not making fun when he leans in to say, "Stick with me, huh? One day at a time."

## Chapter 15

We find Lyn lounging in the library, and she's off the chair before either of us can open our mouths.

"Ghost or no ghost, I'm thinking I might leave you to all of this sooner than later, dear Eve. One or two more days tops for me, and then I've had about as much so-called relaxation as I can stand. Hiya, Nick."

"Hey, Lyn. So, you've seen the ghost? Eve was just telling me about her."

"No, I wish. I was looking for her a little earlier. Eve said she looks like me, so I went around looking for someone who looked like Eve." She smiles at her own joke.

"Wait, the ghost looks like you?" Nick asks, looking at me.

"Yeah, I guess. I thought it was Lyn from far away, but the way she walked . . . I could tell it wasn't her."

Nick stares off, his gaze growing distant.

"Uh, Nick? You okay? Care to share?" I ask, snapping my fingers in front of him and smiling. I'm so glad it's not just me who dazes every once in a while.

"Huh? Oh, yes! I'm fine. Sorry," Nick sheepishly looks from me to Lyn. "I, uh, was thinking about one of my clients."

"They have problems with ghosts that look like them?" Lyn supplies with a grin.

"No, Miss Annoying," Nick said, returning her grin. "Don't worry about it. My business. Let's go to lunch."

It's only when we reach the front porch that I realize my error. When they were handing out the award for idiot of the year, I picked up first, second, and third place prizes. How could I possibly go out to lunch somewhere with a barrier of water between me and it? I'm proud of my little successes on the bridge, but that's exactly what they are—little successes. This though, this is huge.

I must have clenched Nick's hand because he stops and looks down at me. "What's the problem? Did you forget something?"

My breath hitches as my eyes take in the boat at the end of the dock, lifting and swaying with the ripples in the water. "I forgot how much I hate water," I choke as I tremble.

"Hey, hey!" Nick grabs both my shoulders. "Look at me," he commands, and when I do, he's exaggerating his breathing in and out at regular intervals. I follow his lead and begin to feel better. "Are you ok? I was hoping you'd kind of forget that part. You didn't mention it, so I wasn't going to."

"You have a mallet to knock me out? Or you could just use your hand. Be gentle though. I bruise easily." I close my eyes as if waiting for a blow and then open them again. "You know, a pill would probably be better. Yeah, I'd appreciate that more than a lump on the head, please."

Lyn rolls her eyes and crosses her arms against her chest, but I can see she's trying to hide a grin. I understand. I want to laugh right along with her at this insane situation, even though a bigger part of me wants to curl into the fetal position. Nick's eyes narrow in thought. "Your fear is going to make it a bit difficult then, isn't it?" He looks around and then takes my hand. "Let's just try to go down to the dock. Do you think you can do that? You can turn around whenever you want."

Feeling silly, I let out a shaky laugh. "Yes, I can do that. I've been to the water's edge. It's beautiful. I just can't go in it."

We walk down the steps and across the yard toward the water. As we walk, I feel more and more embarrassed and stupid. How else did I think I was going to leave Lakeview? On a plane? I try to let go of my insecurity as I take one deep breath after another, Nick's hand in mine, and the dock getting closer and closer with each step. *I can do this. I can* do *this.*

Once I get to the dock, I stop. I can't do this.

"Just breathe," Nick suggests as he takes a deep breath of his own. "I want you to take a look at the dock. Just look at the dock, the wood boards, the sturdy wood boards."

I do as Nick says and focus on the wooden planks in front of me. They're weathered gray, but I can still see the grain on each board, and the darker colored knots, where branches were cut off, scattered haphazardly before my eyes.

"Can you take a step onto the dock?" Nick asks gently. He continues to hold my hand, and I'm grateful he's not trying to persuade me with a push or a tug.

I place one foot onto the dock and feel the strength of the wood beneath my shoe. Inhaling, I place my other foot on the dock as well.

"That's great! Eve, that's great!" exclaims Nick. "Can you do it again?"

This must be what I felt like upon taking my first steps. There's pride and determination, but there's also the threat of failure and the fear of what could happen. Pushing myself, I put one foot in front of the other, again and again, my breathing jagged, my heart hammering, and my palm sweaty next to Nick's. "I'm doing it!" I yelp.

"You are killing it, Eve! Keep on going, you're almost there."

And maybe saying that was a mistake because that's when I look up to see how far away the boat is, but of course, when I look up to see the boat, I also see the water, the sun reflecting on a wave and blinding me momentarily. I stumble and Nick quickly pulls me into his arms.

I start to cry uncontrollably, and I hate that I'm crying because I'm pissed. At this moment, the only thing I want to do is get on the damn boat and go have some friggin' lunch. I want to be around people who are probably only thinking of their stupid jobs or their stupid lives, and I want to be one of them. I growl in frustration because, despite my anger, my fear is worse.

"It's okay, Eve," Lyn says as she rubs my back.

"No, it's not. I can do this! I *have* to do this. I can't live this way."

"Eve . . ." I can sense Lyn and Nick communicating silently over my bowed head and tear-filled eyes.

"Okay, then. Let's do this. It's on!" I peek at Lyn through my fingers and she's got a look of determination on her face, her free hand balled into a fist. One thing about Lyn: she's always had my back. I smile at her gratefully.

"Yeah, take that—you, you water!" Nick's look of mock anger and the fist he's waving toward the lake have me giggling, and I relax slightly. We stand there for a few moments, my breaths coming easier when Nick lifts my chin. "I know you don't know me from Adam—or Tom, Joe or Louis—" Again I laugh, and Nick smiles. "But Eve, do you trust me?"

Instantly, my fingers dig into his biceps where I clutch pathetically. Apparently not. But then, how can I? I know Lyn's standing here with us, and she wouldn't let him do anything that she didn't trust, but fear defies logic.

"Eve, we have two options, and I'm going to leave it up to you. Are you listening?"

I can't find my voice, so I nod, my body still trembling as I cling to him, my life preserver.

"We can either go to the boat, which is about five more steps, or we can turn around right now and go back to the house."

"H-h-ho-how f-f-f-far is th-th-the g-g-gr-ground?" I manage to get out around my terror.

The hesitation worries me before the words even fall from his mouth. "It's about seven or eight steps, Eve," he says, and I dissolve into tears again.

"Okay, it's okay. We're going to move slowly. It'll be okay. Let's just turn arou—"

"No!" The command is out of my mouth before I can even figure out what I mean by it, but standing here, I know I have to try. Swiping angrily at the tears coursing down my face, I look into Nick's eyes. "I w-w-want t-t-to go to lunch."

He flashes me a delighted smile before standing me up straight, waiting for me to balance on my own two feet, and moving away slightly to act as support rather than as a crutch. My eyes move away from his face and go immediately to the strong, silent strength of the boards below me. We can do this. *I* can do this.

Taking a deep breath, I focus on the boat. I'm so close I can see the white leather seats inside, the silver wheel with white leather grips against the instrument panel. It's all right there in front of me. All I have to do is move my feet. One foot in front of the other. That's all I need to do. I clench the hand not holding onto Nick into a fist, square my shoulders, and promptly faint.

\*\*\*

I wake up on the porch swing. My head is on Nick's shoulder as he sits beside me, his hand still holding mine.

"I guess you forgot to breathe," Nick supplies as he caresses my hand.

I jump up and immediately feel dizzy enough to sit back down, putting my head between my knees. After a few moments, I slowly sit back up and turn to Nick.

"Lyn?" I ask. It's all I need to say.

"She went inside, said something about all the excitement wearing her out."

"I am so sorry," I say, wondering what the protocol is for fainting before going out to lunch with a good-looking guy one hardly knows.

Nick smirks. "You could have just told me you didn't want to go." The tone of his voice and the look in his eyes make it sound as if we were going on a date instead of just out to lunch. After all, Lyn was going too.

I nudge him with my shoulder, "And miss out on all that fun?"

"Yeah, so much fun. I think my arms almost came out of their sockets the way you were pulling on them."

I cringe. "Nick, really, I'm so, so—"

"I'm kidding, Eve. It's called lightening the mood. You have nothing to be sorry for."

"Why didn't you just put me on the boat? I could have woken up to a juicy hamburger."

"I'm no expert, but I think you have to face your fears. If I had put you on that boat, it would have been cheating," Nick says. His hand rests on my arm with a comforting weight.

I stand up, walk to the edge of the porch, and look down toward the water and to the boat at the end of the dock. From here, there's not even an inkling of fear. I watch the boat gently sway back and forth and I know I can find peace down there if I could just get past this barrier that's holding me back. "Can we try it again, another time?" I ask, determination and hope vying for dominance.

"Of course!" Nick chimes in right away. "But next time, can you trim your fingernails before we go?" He winces as he rubs his biceps before breaking into another grin.

"Maybe next time, I'll just push you in instead," I smirk back, and I'm happy because there is no weirdness. It's just Nick and me and a shared experience, even if it wasn't lunch.

## Chapter 16

**I**'m still sitting on the front porch, Nick having left about a half-hour ago, when Ari comes out through the front door.

"Hi," he says when he sees me. Then, "I was expecting someone else."

I laugh, remembering it's exactly what I said when we met in the hall. "I didn't mean to sneak up on you," I say, echoing his words.

He comes over to sit next to me. "Are you okay?"

I wrap my arms around myself and give a small nod. "When I was little, my parents bought something really big that came in a box. Maybe it was a refrigerator; at least, the box was big enough for a refrigerator. Anyway, I asked for the box and spent so much time in it. I cut a window into it and would go in there to read books and hide away, especially when Lyn had people over to play. 'Come out and live life,' my mom would say, but I was content hanging out in there, a part of everything but separate. Then, when I knew enough about what was going on, I would come out and play."

Ari doesn't say anything while I talk, but I can almost see his mind working, trying to figure out why I'm telling him one of my memories.

"Boxes can be fun, but sometimes they can feel claustrophobic, don't you think?" he asks, tilting his head.

I consider it for a minute. "Didn't Hamlet say something about living in a nutshell and considering himself the king of infinite space?"

Ari nods. "I guess it depends on if there's anyone else in there with you," he says. "Why are you telling me this, Eve?"

"Because I was thinking of it just now, the box I played with. In some ways, this house reminds me of that box. I'm in my own little world here, and you're just a figment of my imagination in my little box with me. You and Nick both."

Ari is silent for a moment as the swing rocks back and forth with slight pushes from our feet. "Let's assume we're in your little box," Ari suggests. "You said you would go to hide away. What are you hiding from, Eve?"

"Have you ever been afraid of something?"

"You mean like things that go bump in the night or something more substantial, like monsters and werewolves?"

I nudge him with my shoulder and smile before saying, "Today when Lyn and I were about to go out to lunch with Nick, I fainted."

"Ahh, you're afraid of Nick. Understandable," Ari says, nodding, and I laugh.

"I'm afraid of the water," I announce. "Isn't it strange? I mean, I know lots of people have a fear of water. That's not what's strange, but how did I get here if I'm afraid of water? Why don't I remember, and why doesn't Lyn remember, either?" I don't mention my suspicion that she does remember or the reason she wants me to remember on my own.

"You think that's what you're hiding from?"

"It could be. Anyway . . ." I look at him and smile. "Thanks for listening."

"I enjoy talking to you." We sit for a while, and I notice how our fingers are only inches apart. Ari must notice as well because he ever so slowly edges his closer until our pinkies are touching. His voice is hesitant when he says, "Um, I have to ask you something, and I'll be completely fine with your answer, either way, so don't think you have to sugarcoat anything for my benefit, okay?"

I swallow thickly. The consternation in his voice giving me pause. "What's up?"

"This thing with Nick . . . I don't want to get in his way or yours." Ari pulls his fingers away from mine, and his voice lowers. "You said you couldn't go, and I know you must have been disappointed and probably most of that is because you couldn't get off the island, but if some of it was because you wanted to go with Nick, well, yeah, I'm rambling now."

"I am disappointed I couldn't go, and I'd be lying if I told you a part of me didn't want to go because of Nick, but I also feel drawn to this place—drawn to you in a way I can't explain. I want to get to know you too." I can feel my heart beating inside my chest. I have rarely talked about my feelings to people I barely know, and sitting on the porch and confessing this to Ari just seems so intimate.

"If you want to get to know me, why'd you say no to going out?" Ari moves his hand back next to mine and traps my little finger with his. I inhale sharply and impulsively want to pull away. I blame it on the shock of his sudden movement, but in the back of my head, there's a bit of revulsion. *Why?*

"I guess it's just . . ." I trail off, at a loss for how to tell him he scares me, even though there's nothing else to do but give it to him straight.

"Go ahead, Eve. Just tell me. What is it?"

I stand, partly to move away and partly to see him better, and face him. "You scare me," I blurt out.

He looks down but not fast enough to hide the sadness and disappointment I see clearly etched on his face.

"That sounds so stupid, I know. You've been nothing but kind to me, and I don't know why . . . I mean, you're attractive, funny; you listen to what I say. I'm . . . I don't know."

There's a sparkle in his eyes when he looks up. "You think I'm attractive?"

"I say you scare me and *that's* what you choose to focus on?"

"There's so much negativity in the world," Ari says dramatically, throwing his arms wide for effect.

I can't help but chuckle.

"That sounded like genuine laughter to me. Are you sure it's *me* you're scared of?"

"What's that supposed to mean?" I want to take offense at what sounds like an intended dig, but deep down, I think he may be right.

"Maybe you fear taking a chance." He flicks an invisible piece of lint off his pant leg.

*Oh, he's good.*

"So, you're trying to use reverse psychology on me so I'll say it's not you who scares me but blame myself instead?"

"Depends . . ."

"On what?"

"If it's working." He looks up at me and hope shines like a beacon from his eyes. It's not the puppy-dog look he promised would get to me; it's a look of promise for what could be if I say yes. At this point, even my instinct to run has fled, my heartbeat only quickened by what seems to be a mutual attraction.

He must see a change in my demeanor because he stands with me and reaches for my hand. "Say yes now—that you'll go out with me. Please?"

He's charming, his finger laced with mine, his eyes hopeful, and his smile gorgeous. I don't want to say no, and besides the teeny tiny voice telling me to—I have no good reason not to. "Okay, yes."

"Yes?" Ari's eyebrows lift and he grants me a smile that radiates warmth and pleasure.

I laugh again and nod.

"Great! I'll, um, I'll ring for you tomorrow. Is seven o'clock good?"

"Aren't you staying here? I can meet you in—"

"Nope, I'm going to do this the right way, ring the doorbell and everything."

"Wow. Should I be impressed?"

Ari stills. "I don't do this"—he gestures between the two of us as he shakes his head— "so I want to make sure I do it correctly."

His words and actions are either romantic . . . or they're proof I should listen to Nick and stay the hell away. But standing here in front of him, totally aware of these conflicting feelings, I have to give in. "Seven is fine."

Ari gives me another breathtaking smile, steps away quickly as if in a hurry to get away from me before I change my mind, and walks to the front door where he stops to turn, his penetrating blue eyes on me. "Thanks, Eve. I'll see you then."

"Unless I see you before then," I say with raised brows. "You know, with you staying—"

"Bye, Eve."

"Bye, Ari."

➤ The House on the Lake

## Chapter 17

It took five tries to find my room last night.

The first time, I was surprised when the door to what I thought was my room felt as if it was blocked. I pushed on it a few times only to see the room of an adolescent. Clothes littered the floor in piles like the one blocking the door, and the single bed against one corner was unmade, the bold-colored sheets haphazardly strewn. Teenage heartthrobs lined the room on posters that seemed glued to the walls, and on a full-length mirror in the distance, curling photos of smiling faces lined the edges. Books from different subjects—math, science, history—sat on a desk covered with papers, an assortment of pens, a couple of mugs, and a radio, and a bookbag was placed next to the chair. I swiftly eyed the hallway to see if a haughty teenager, arms crossed, would stare me down for daring to get too close to her sanctuary, but there was no one.

Closing the door to the room, I looked around. It definitely looked like the hallway where my room was supposed to be. I walked back to the stairs and tried again.

The second time, the door took me to the kitchen. When I walked back up from the kitchen, I was taken to a music room. There weren't many instruments, but the number of records, tapes, and CDs on shelves that lined three walls was overwhelming. A stereo with two large speakers sat on a table against the fourth wall. A microphone and a headset were there too. Although I wanted to stay and sing a song or two, I was growing frustrated with not being able to get to my room, so I hoped I would actually find it again and shut the door.

Then I decided to try to open the door right away, without walking away from it first. When I did, I was greeted with the stairs to the attic. I closed the door again. That the rooms were moving was still exciting—a bit unnerving, to be sure—but I had witnessed it before. What was off was the frequency. I might have had to go searching once or twice for a room, but never this many times, and I'd never had a problem finding my room before. That I was still looking for it was a bit annoying.

I leaned my forehead against the door and with every fiber in my being willed what lay beyond to be my room. My wish probably had nothing to do with it, but when I opened the door again, it was my room, a little darker, a little drabber than it was when I first opened my eyes within its walls, but its presence was still inviting. Thankful, I tumbled onto the bed, and fearing the room would change again if I even tried to go to the bathroom, I lay there and closed my eyes, the irregular sound of what I'd come to think of as the heart of the house lulling me to sleep.

It's cold and dreary outside today, and the chilly, moist air has permeated the house. Whereas a few days ago I wouldn't have thought too much about it, especially with the lake right next to the manor, it's different now. More. I can feel the damp all the way to my bones in practically every room I wander. It drapes itself on all the furniture and hangs heavily in the air. And if before there was a hint of mustiness, the odor is now omnipresent—dank and fetid and mixed with something else. The smell of death.

I can't get Gail's words out of my head. *It's dying.* But I don't see how it's possible. Maybe she means the house is more rundown than it looks, its wood rotting under the pervasive wet air. The mold and mildew within the rooms can attest to the humidity. Would it be so farfetched for her to think of the house as living?

Shivering from the cold air, I wrap my arms around myself as I make my way down one of the countless hallways. Every time I think I've seen all I can see of the house, I find more rooms, more passages. Some corridors lead back to rooms I've visited before, even though I was nowhere near their location to start, just like some of the common rooms let on to halls I've never seen. I feel like I could spend a lifetime here and still be uncertain what would be around the next corner.

And it's unexpected that around the next corner, I run into Ari.

"Hello again," he says, his eyes lighting up in surprised happiness.

"Hi yourself." I grin. His closeness makes me shiver and I'm tempted to take a step back, but then I remember the look in his eyes when I told him he scared me. I don't want to see that look again, knowing I caused it, even if his proximity raises the hair on the back of my neck.

"Having fun poking around?"

My gaze travels up and down the dim hallway, and my brows furrow. *Does he mind my snooping?* "I was told I'm allowed to. I'm not going through anything personal, not opening any drawers or anything."

Ari waves his hand in the air like it's the least of his worries. "Maybe you should," he says.

"What?"

He ignores my question. "You know," he says instead, "people are always trying to find answers—to everything— but a lot of times, they just wonder without attempting to solve the answer. You ever notice that?"

Oh yeah, noticed and been guilty of it. There're too many unknowns not to. I nod.

He leans back on his heels. "So, I never asked, what do you think of the place?"

I hesitate because I like it. I really do. More than like it, but like Lyn, I'm growing tired of the silence, and I'm growing tired of the constant introspection it brings.

"Uh-oh, what's wrong?" Ari asks as he steps toward me, his brows drawn together in concern.

"Nothing! I love it. It's just . . . I'm not used to all the silence," I say as I look everywhere but at him. I dare not look at him, his chiseled jaw, his wide shoulders, the way his jeans hang off his hips in just the right way. Nick was right. Ari's dangerous, but only in the way I feel my attraction for him growing. I can feel his eyes on me, and I feel warmed by them despite the chill in the air. I need to think of something else or I'm going to make a fool of myself by launching into his arms, so I tell him my suspicions. "And to tell you the truth, I think it's haunted."

He doesn't act surprised and there's amusement in his eyes, a small smile playing around his lips, as if he could hear my thoughts and was waiting to see if I'd act on them. "Really? Who do you think is haunting it?"

"No, the house itself is haunted."

Ari nods, thinking about my words. "I'm generally a skeptic myself," he says. "I think there's always an explanation for what's happening, however strange it may be."

"Maybe." I concede, "but there's so much going on here."

"Then find the answers. They're here somewhere, most likely."

"Aren't you even curious?"

Ari's eyes pierce mine, and he leans toward me, the small smile still there. "Trust me, Eve, there're tons of things I'd love to know about this place," he says. His voice is a caress and I feel a chill go up my spine. He must know he's affecting me; I don't see how he couldn't, but he steps back casually, languidly. "But I've got work to do. Perhaps you can figure it out for me?"

"Are you going to tell me I can steal something next?" I ask with a twinkle in my eye.

Ari smiles. "I would never condone stealing, but snooping around, I don't see why not. It's not like the owner has any state secrets to hide."

"So, I can blame you if the owner finds out and wants to press charges?"

He throws his head back and laughs, a throaty, deep laugh that vibrates through my body. "I take full responsibility." He turns to walk away but hesitates. "We're still good for tonight, right? Seven o'clock?"

There's a vulnerability in his gaze and again, he hides his eyes before I can read too much. It's endearing, this soft side of him, when his physicality shows so much strength.

I smile shyly and nod.

Ari smiles too. "Snoop away, Eve."

➤ The House on the Lake

## Chapter 18

◆———————•———————◆

**I** can't find Lyn, so I decide to go up in the attic once more. When I reach the top of the stairs, all is quiet. My eyes rest for a moment on the picture above the fireplace before they travel around the room slowly. My senses are heightened; my eyes spot dust motes in the air and my ears pick up on all the normal groans, thuds, and creaks associated with an old house. I blame my uneasiness on my scare up here the other day and straighten my shoulders. I'm determined to find some answers, and an echo of Ari's words replay in my mind: *Snoop away, Eve.*

Stepping forward, my first objective is to open all the curtains to let in as much light as possible. On the way, I shake my fist at my reflection in the damned mirror that nearly scared me to death and laugh under my breath. I won't be scared by that again.

Soft sunlight filters through the filthy panes as I throw back the curtains, and I raise my shirt over my nose while trying to open one of the windows to let in some fresh air.

Only one budges a few inches, and I squat so my nose is level with the cool breeze. I allow my shirt to drop and take a few deep breaths while rising to take in the scenery. Unlike the blocked view of the last window, the view from this one shows more of the lake. From here, I could swear the house is suspended above the water, and for a moment, I feel dizzy—not by the height, but by the sheer volume of liquid I know surrounds me. Inhaling to calm myself, a musty, dank scent invades my nostrils. My nose wrinkles at the smell. It's not enough to have me backtracking to the stairs, but it's enough for me to sneeze a couple of times. I try to lift the window a bit more but soon give up and turn to the reason I'm up here in the first place. The boxes I looked through the other day are, of course, where they were before, and moving aside the ones filled with the swimming trophies, I squat and unfold the flaps of another.

It's an assortment of trinkets.

There are various glass figurines, each individually wrapped in tissue paper. Unwrapping the first unveils a small, transparent deer that fits in the palm of my hand; another uncovers a transparent unicorn with a golden horn of approximately the same size. I unwrap several others before surmising the owner is a collector. I place all the tissue-wrapped items to one side and look at what else is in the box.

A square, blue velvet case catches my attention, and I set it on my knee while I return the tissue-wrapped figurines. Once finished, I open the case to find a small, tarnished heart-shaped locket on an equally tarnished Figaro chain. Fumbling with the small latch, it takes several tries to open the locket. I see two tiny pictures inserted on either side. They're faded and blurry, so I can't make out the faces of those who may or may not be long dead. *Who are you? Why are you hiding?* A distinct silence answers my questioning thoughts. It feels heavy, like even those in the photographs hanging on the walls are waiting with bated breath for the answer.

I fold the chain and start to put it back inside its case, and because everything is so quiet, the whisper of a sound hits my ears. I still, afraid to turn around. *It's gotta be Lyn.* But my mouth is suddenly dry, and I swallow to slow my breath, which is increasing despite my efforts to calm down. Another, closer sound hits my ears: a chair scraping on the floor. I try to swallow again, but my throat is too tight. "Lyn?" Her name is a hoarse whisper that's met with a *creak, swish… creak, swish.*

My legs, already tired from squatting, give out on me and I land on my butt. I scramble to stand and turn around at the same time, debating whether to look at the source of the noise or to race past it. My heart is pounding in my chest and

I want to run, but I don't want to wonder either. What if it's just my imagination?

I glance up quickly at first, then lower my eyes immediately. There's something there. There's *someone* there. Sitting in the rocking chair, which slowly moves back and forth *creak, swish… creak, swish*. I stop breathing. Slowly I raise my eyes again, seeing but not registering anything until I get to her face . . . or where her face should be. Instead, her image is blurred. It's as if a filter of murky water has suddenly been thrown over my eyes. I can see, but everything is distorted, moving when it should be standing still.

I can still hear the distinct *creak, swish* of the chair, its tempo changing, getting faster. My heart beats in time as my breath comes back to me in ragged pants. I search for her eyes, but every time I believe there to be a clearing of my vision, everything becomes blurry once more.

"Who are you?" I whisper, but instead of an answer, an overwhelming sense of sadness envelops me. Blinking rapidly, my vision clears enough for me to see her move a hand to clutch the arm of the chair. *She's going to get up.* I brace myself for what she's about to do—

The window I opened earlier slams shut, arresting my heart for a few beats but also loosening me from my trance. My head whips to the window and I blink a few times, trying to get my bearings before returning my gaze to the rocker and the ghost.

My eyesight has returned.

But the chair is empty, and the ghost is gone.

➤ The House on the Lake

## Chapter 19

I rush through the house, glancing in rooms, in search of Lyn. A room-to-room telephone system would work wonders in this place, but even if I knew what room she was in, there's no way to know if I'd find the room. They still keep changing. And again, I had trouble finding my own room when I left the attic. After my encounter, a sweater was definitely in order, and even after tearing up one hall and down another looking for Lyn, I still can't stop the tremors that run through my body.

"Hey, whatcha doin'?" Lyn asks as I scurry into the kitchen. I'm not really expecting to find her here, so I'm caught off guard when I see her standing next to Nick and across from Gail and Hammond, all of them with polite smiles on their faces. I've interrupted something and suddenly feel I should turn around and walk back out.

I wonder if they're discussing the woman I've seen or my teleportation trick, but it's obvious they were discussing me. Hammond is suddenly studying the crown molding and

Gail is back to worrying her fingers, glancing at anything but me. Nick leans into Lyn, says something I can't hear, and puts his arm around her shoulders, squeezing her for a moment. A twinge of jealousy shoots through me, and I quickly look down at my shoes. I don't want Lyn feeling sorry for me, and I don't want Nick feeling bad for choosing Lyn.

At the moment, I'm not even sure exactly who I'm jealous of: Lyn for getting the attention of a good-looking, seemingly nice guy or Nick for being so close to Lyn.

And both scenarios strike me as weird. Nick is great, but since I've met Ari, he's who my thoughts stray to, and I've never been one to want the attention of a man just for the sake of having it. As for Lyn, I've always been close to her, so I don't know why I would feel so insecure about someone else being close to her too. Whatever prompts this emotion, I feel like I'm missing out on something, and the jealousy leaves me with a bitter taste. It's just something else I'll have to piece together.

"Um, I have to go. I have business to attend to," Nick says, and I smile, remembering Ari echoing his brother. Nick stands in front of me and his vivid green eyes, so different from Ari's blue, capture mine. "Let's try to go out for lunch later. You up to it?"

In the second it takes for me to answer him, I think about how I feel. Accepted. Acknowledged. I feel a part of something I've always wanted to be part of. Nick has that kind of draw, so even though I've agreed to go out with Ari later tonight, I give a little nod and glance at Lyn to see how she's taking our interaction. There's no reproach in her gaze, no hurt, and I'm glad.

But I still somehow feel like a bitch. What the hell am I doing?

"Great! I'll see you both then." With a backward glance at Lyn and a smile to me, he practically glides out the door.

"He's such a vibrant man," sighs Gail.

"I'm glad you're going out to lunch with him," adds Hammond in a matter-of-fact tone and a curt nod to boot. "I only foresee good things if you were to stick with that one."

"Oh! I forgot to talk to him about—" startles Gail as she loses her smile and concern creases her brow.

Hammond presses his hand against her lower back, essentially leading and pushing her out the door at the same time. "We can catch up to him. Don't worry yourself even more. Let's go."

Lyn shakes her head as they leave the room and then pretends to tidy up and fails miserably since there are no props to help her. Instead, she swipes her hand across the clean counter, depositing imaginary crumbs into the sink.

"What were you talking about before I came in?" I ask point-blank.

"Oh, Eve, it's not all about you if that's what you're thinking."

"I wasn't exactly born yesterday, you know. You could cut the tension in here with a knife when I walked in. Is it you and Nick?"

"Me and—" Lyn's eyebrows raise in surprise. "Oh, geez, Eve, no! Is that what that little look was about? You're jealous?"

My silence propels her to repeat herself. "No." She shakes her head. "Just, no. He's nice and cute—oh, who am I kidding, the man's hot!" We both laugh. "It's just . . ." She shakes her head again. "He's friendly, he's cool, but I just want a ride back to the mainland. But *you* . . ." She searches my eyes. "Why don't you go after him?"

I lean against the counter and think about what I want. When I first saw Nick, I was mesmerized by him, tongue-tied even, and I feel like he's the brother I should want. After all, Lyn gets along well with him and Gail raves about him, and he's genuinely a nice guy, but something's changed. And Ari has everything to do with it.

"I met Nick's brother," I tell her. "We've talked a few times, and he wants to meet up later tonight. You'd like him, Lyn."

It takes a long time for Lyn to answer, and when she does, it's as if she's choosing her words carefully. "You know, if you're not interested in Nick, just say so. I'm not trying to push you. You don't have to make things up."

My eyes widen. "Why would you think I'm making him—Lyn, I'm *not* making him up!" I glare at her as I stand up straight.

"So, you saw him like you saw the woman you were talking about? Did you actually have a conversation with him, or did he disappear on you?"

"Yes, I did have a conversation with him, thank you very much. I just said that, and I like him. I don't know why Nick said what he did about him."

"Who's a nice guy?" Gail asks as she comes back into the kitchen carrying a bucket of water.

"Ari," I state, and she stumbles forward, some water sloshing out of the bucket.

Gail regains her footing and continues toward the sink slowly, emptying the bucket. "You met Ari then," she says, her tone neutral.

"Yes. What, you don't believe me either?"

"No, no. It's not that." Gail sets the bucket on the floor next to her and stares out the window, her shoulders drooping.

"What's wrong with Ari? Why are you acting like he's some horrible person? Has he killed someone or something?"

Gail coughs and picks the bucket up once again. "There's nothing *wrong* with Ari, per se," she says as she walks back to the door. "He's . . . well, he's Ari, is all." And with that, she's gone again.

"I'm sorry," Lyn mumbles. "I should have listened to you. I thought you were just trying to get attention."

"What, why?" If anyone has ever sought attention, it's Lyn, not me.

"It's just all these bizarre things keep happening to you. Why? How come I haven't seen the woman? And I walked through the side door like twenty times, yet I never ended up on the porch—although yeah, the rooms moving locations is pretty freaky—and now you've met Ari too."

I nod. I get it. I've been asking myself the same questions, but wanting attention and wanting to talk about some considerably strange things are two totally different things.

"So, are you going to tell me more about him?"

"There's not much to tell. I don't know him that well."

184

"But you want to." Lyn nods, a grin on her face when she sees me smile.

"He seems nice," I say, "and there's something kind of mysterious about him, but I don't know if I've just let what Nick and Gail are saying get under my skin, you know? It's like, when I talk to him, sometimes I want to run as far as I can in the opposite direction, just get away from him, and I feel all panicky, like he's going to pull a gun from behind his back or something." I laugh. "But then, most of the time, I feel this draw to him. It's similar to my draw for Nick but so much *more*, and I can't help staring at him—you think Nick's hot—whew!" Lyn snorts as I fan myself. "And I want to keep staring at him," I continue, "but I don't want him to think I'm this weirdo."

"Too late for that. You *are* a weirdo," Lyn laughs as she punches me in the shoulder.

"Shut up."

"I'm kidding. You know I love you, stalker potential and all."

My smile falters. "Nick is great, but from what I can tell, Ari is too."

"Yeah, I hear you. But just keep in mind that you don't know him. Nick and Gail do. From what I can tell—even after the way Gail yelled at you—they genuinely seem to want what's best for you. Do you think they would steer you wrong just to spite you?"

I know Lyn's right, but I can't help myself. Anyway, how well do I know Nick and Gail? Everyone seems to have the best of intentions, but even I've heard the old saying about the road to hell being paved with them. I can only follow what I feel. And now that I've met Ari, I don't know if I want to walk away. There's no doubt there's an attraction between us, and although I can't guarantee that a part of it might be because I've been warned away from him, an even bigger part is because I'm falling for him. Hard.

I leave the kitchen without answering, and my reason for finding Lyn—to tell her about the ghost in the attic— takes a backseat as my thoughts linger on Ari and everything I don't know.

# Chapter 20

I'm sitting on the front porch steps when Ari comes from the side of the house.

"Hey! What are you doing out here? I said I was going to ring the doorbell."

"This house is so big, who knows if I'd even hear the doorbell," I say with a smile as I stand to greet him. "Anyway, I can just picture Hammond answering the door and giving you the third degree about your intentions, so if you think about it, I saved you."

Ari smiles. "Thank you. You're right. Seeing Hammond's face is not the way I would want to start this evening." He fakes a shudder. "But I still want to do this correctly. If that means I have to face Hammond or Gail, I will."

"It's okay. You're off the hook," I say, suddenly shy. I don't really know this man, and now that's he's standing in front of me, I have no idea what we're going to talk about for the evening.

"I'm glad." He takes a few steps toward me so we're only a couple of feet apart. "You look beautiful by the way."

I blush and shift my focus to anywhere but him. "Thank you," I say, and then to save us from any awkward silences, I ask about this evening. "So, what did you have in mind for tonight?"

"Have you eaten?" Ari asks. "We could go to the kitchen and I can whip up a mean sandwich depending on what's in the refrigerator."

I shake my head. "We can go if you want, but I'm not that hungry."

"Don't women eat, or is it you just don't eat in front of men you don't know very well? How does that work exactly?"

I laugh. "Trust me, when I'm hungry, the world knows it, especially when there's a BLT pizza from my favorite pizzeria on the line. I don't care if I've just met you or not."

"Good. I don't want you to hide from me, Eve." His blue eyes caress my face, and I feel my cheeks flush once again. I'm pretty sure he sees it because he takes a couple of steps back and looks up at the house. "You know, I'm not really hungry either. How about we take a look at a part of the house you probably haven't explored yet?"

I light up, instantly intrigued. "Really? Okay, cool." I think about the doors I haven't been able to open and wonder if Ari has the keys. If he and Nick are planning on selling the place or closing it down or whatever, I guess they would need them.

"Have you checked out the basement yet?" Ari asks as he holds out his hand for me.

My hand jumps to my chest and dark tales of Edgar Allan Poe begin to fill my head. "I have to say, I never thought about going into the basement," I admit tentatively. "Why would we go there?"

"No, I have no devious plans," Ari says as he holds up his hands innocently. "I know it's an odd place to ask someone to go, but basements can be filled with all sorts of secrets and treasure. We can ask Gail or Hammond to go if you want a chaperone."

Every time I start to get creeped out by something he says or does or how he looks at me, he says or does something or looks at me differently to make me change my mind. Based on that alone, I know I should turn around and not look back, but in this case, I don't want to run.

"It must be one of the doors that's locked," I say, "because I've seriously tried every door in this place." I realize I sound like a major snoop, but hey, it's who I am. I might as well put myself out there. I won't be on this island forever, and I'll never get anywhere unless I let my little light shine.

Ari doesn't seem offended by my confession. "You'll have to tell me what you've found out about this place," he says, and I take heart in knowing that if this all goes south, it's not due to my curiosity.

I wait for him to lead the way, but he stands as if he's waiting for me to do the same. "Are you okay?" I ask.

"Yup, I'm following your lead."

"But . . . I don't know where I'm going."

Ari smiles. "Makes it all the more interesting, doesn't it? I'll be with you the whole time. I promise."

"Wait, so, we're going to the basement, and even though I have no idea how to get there, you're just going to let me wander aimlessly until I stumble upon it?" My voice may sound incredulous, but on the inside, I'm bouncing up and down like I just won exclusive rights to the Winchester mystery house.

Ari laughs and spreads his arms, "It's yours while you're here. Lead the way!"

# Chapter 21

We wander through the house and I do see places I've never seen before, which I find fascinating. It looks like I have more exploring to do. As we go, I point out some of the rooms I find especially comforting—the kitchen, the library, the music room. Ari asks questions while we walk and seems genuinely interested when I answer.

I'm feeling so comfortable and at ease that I start to worry something's wrong. Is it supposed to be this easy? Shouldn't there be more angst and inner turmoil? I'm with a man people have warned me against. Even my own body has instinctually pulled away from him at times, yet right now, it's as if nothing could be more natural than being with him.

I throw my hands in the air. "I give up. You're going to have to tell me where it is. We've been everywhere."

"We didn't try upstairs."

"We're looking for the basement. I've never heard of a basement being above the ground floor."

"Sometimes you have to go up to go down."

"That sounds like I song I used to hear."

Ari grins. "Well, maybe there's some logic in it, then."

"I doubt it, but let's go." I lead him to the second floor via the grand staircase with the stained glass window. It's only now I notice a thick layer of dust and grime coating the multicolored pieces. It's dark outside, and no light streams through from the sky. Instead, the interior is lit with wall sconces and an overhead hanging light above the staircase.

When we get to the hidden door of the attic, I tell Ari about it and how I almost scared myself to death by looking in the mirror. I don't tell him about the ghost in the chair.

Ari laughs, shaking his head. "I'm sure there's some deep, psychological meaning in there if you want to think about it."

"Not really. I mean, you're probably right, but I don't want to think about it."

"Why not?"

"Because seeing myself almost had me screaming. I don't want to think about what that means psychologically. Am I scared of myself? Do I believe myself to be a bad person? Have I repressed some dark secret I'm afraid to unveil? If it doesn't come to me naturally, I don't know if I should go poking around trying to figure out what it is. I think I prefer to live in ignorance."

Ari nods. "Understood. Just remember that the truth has a way of making itself known." He wiggles his fingers and eyebrows but his teasing can't hide the veracity of his words. My heart beats faster, and my breathing is a little bit quicker. The hall even seems to be longer than it was minutes ago, and I wonder what the hell I'm hiding from myself.

I think Ari notices how uncomfortable I am. Of course, the fact that I've stopped in the middle of the hallway might have something to do with it. He puts his arm around my shoulder and squeezes. "Where to next?"

I'm thankful. His question brings me back to the present, and I notice we're standing next to my bedroom door. "Was this all a ploy to get me to my bedroom?" I joke.

Ari's blue eyes glitter with possibilities and he lifts my chin, staring at my lips and then into my eyes. His dark hair falls onto his forehead as he leans in. I feel an incredible urge to run my fingers through his hair, to touch him. At the same time, that voice—that tiny voice—at the back of my mind tells me to stop, to turn around, to run in the opposite direction.

The air is filled with a tension that wasn't there a moment ago, and my body struggles with the temptation before me.

"Eve," Ari breathes against my ear, "who said what happens between you and me requires a bedroom?"

My breath hitches, and I take a step back only to step forward again, closer to him. I may be a little afraid right now, but I've also never felt so unbelievably attracted to another person. I don't know if he's making a promise or giving me a warning.

Yes, there's something about Ari that screams mystery and danger, and more and more, I think it's an intangible feeling associated with Ari himself rather than any jealous warnings of his brother I've subconsciously incorporated. It's true, Ari has only ever been pleasant and polite, but there's an undercurrent of intrigue I've yet to puzzle out.

"Well, as you can see, there's nothing here, no stairs," I say when he follows me in.

He doesn't say anything and instead strides over to one of the walls and leans against it as he looks around.

"That goes to the bathroom." I point to one of the doors. "And that one—" I point to the door he's leaning next to, "—goes to the closet."

"Interesting."

"Not really." I sag down onto my bed and look at him. "Why don't you just tell me where it is?"

Ari shifts, moving so he's in front of the door and directly across from me. "You don't strike me as the type to give up." He rests his head on the door and closes his eyes. And I watch him.

All of a sudden it hits me how much I've been talking, how much he has been listening. "You're quiet." I wait for a sign of boredom, a yawn to give him away.

"Am I?" His eyes open, sharp and penetrating, as if he knows what I'm thinking while the thoughts form, and he's waiting to see what I'll think next. He's not bored. He's intrigued, just like me.

I breathe an internal sigh of relief. "You don't like talking." I realize that now. Normally, I'm the same way, just taking everything in, being in the moment. I always let Lyn do all the chatting. When we were little, she was the first one to talk. She was the show, and I was the audience.

"I enjoy listening to you."

"You do?" I smile as he nods, and he pushes off the door and sits next to me on the bed. I'm nervous because I don't want to hear that nagging voice in the background telling me Ari is bad. That I need to get away.

At least, that's what I tell myself because his proximity and the scent of his aftershave have nothing to do with it.

I lick my lips. It's not like I've never kissed a guy, but it's never been like this. I've never been a bundle of nerves before. I'm lying. Of course, I've been. It's a kiss, but normally when this moment arrives, I just let it happen. I don't shy away from it. Kisses are like that. They hang over me. I need to get the anticipation out of the way, and I can never fully get comfortable until that first one is over.

This time is different. It's like I want to draw out the anticipation as long as possible, like there's some sort of inevitability connecting us and this is just the beginning, and it's a beginning I want but desperately need to prolong at the same time. I don't even know if that makes sense. Regardless, more words spew from my mouth. "Half the time, I feel like I'm rambling. Tell me a little about you."

"Because I'm that mysterious." He waves his fingers in the universal spooky manner.

My eyes narrow. "You are in some ways."

Ari looks to the floor for a moment and then at me. "What do you want to know?"

"I don't know." Of course, all the questions I have go flying from my mind when he asks. "Just tell me something about yourself."

The corners of his mouth turn up. "I'm not a big talker."

I throw a pillow at him, and he laughs.

"I'm being serious," I say, the nervousness I felt moments ago gone.

"I know," he replies. "I'll tell you what, I promise that one day, I'll answer all your questions, maybe some you never knew you had."

I raise an eyebrow. "Wow, you think I'm *that* curious about you? Well, just based on that last comment alone, I guess I learned something else."

"Oh yeah, what's that?"

"Your ego is the size of this island!"

Ari pushes me over on the bed and starts to tickle me. I haven't felt this carefree in a long while, and it feels good. Damn good. I laugh, twisting and turning to avoid his pokes to my sides and under my arms, and suddenly I'm not laughing anymore because he's hovering over me, his hair touching my forehead, his focus on my eyes, my lips.

"Can I borrow something? I promise I'll give it right back." His voice is a purr; I can feel the vibrations on my skin, and I almost don't realize he's asking me for something.

I tilt my head, my brows furrowed. "Ahh, sure. What?"

"This," he says, and he kisses me. It's soft and warm and wonderful, and the moment is not long enough. Too soon, he breaks the kiss, his eyes still intent on mine.

If I could capture this moment and replay it over and over again, I would. If I could stop time, it would stop right when my lips and his touched. My eyes wander over his face, lingering on his mouth, and I touch my fingers to his cheek. I want him to kiss me again, but that little voice is back, insistent, telling me to back off.

"You're *such* a cheese bag," I say. My voice is husky even to my ears, but for better or worse, my words are lame enough to shatter the moment.

"I know," he says with a grin and a wink. "And now you know two more things about me. That, and" —he kisses me again before sitting up— "the fact that I keep my promises."

I'm in one of those happy dazes as I sit up, and when I finally register that he's looking at me with one of his knowing smirks, I blurt out the first thing that comes to me to throw him off the fact that I'm totally crushing on him right now. "I think I know where the basement is."

Ari gets off the bed. "My kisses are that good, huh?"

I head to the closet, tossing over my shoulder, "Is the island getting bigger? Because your ego sure is."

Ari cocks his head to the side. "Yeah, okay, I deserved that one. So, where is the basement then?"

I open the closet door and move toward the back. The first day I was here, I noticed a small knob on what looked like some painted plywood. I assumed it was just access to the attic and hadn't thought much of it, not even after Lyn and I found the actual attic.

The door opens with a click and the bottom lightly scrapes the wooden floor. I try to lift the door as it swings on its hinges to make sure I don't leave any scratches and glance at Ari for reassurance that we're allowed to do this. I feel as if we're breaking and entering and keep forgetting I've been given free rein over the house and grounds. I don't know if that right is extended to secret passageways, but it was okay with the attic, so I'm just going to assume the same applies here.

As I'm thinking about this, I also cower because I'm expecting bats to come out like in the movies. When none come flying out, I straighten, elbowing Ari because he's laughing at me, and peer into the darkness. I allow my eyes to adjust and can see small, dim sconces every few feet. There are no stairs but a narrow, gradual descent. The smell of damp, musty earth hits my nose, and I'm about to sneeze, which I squelch by rubbing it before moving forward.

"Can you see?" asks Ari from behind me.

"Yeah, I'm good," I say as I continue, my steps becoming faster as my eyes become more and more accustomed to my surroundings. "This is so cool. I feel like I'm in an *Indiana Jones* movie or something."

I come to a bend and slow down, peeking around it before cautiously moving forward.

"What's the matter?" Ari peers over my head to see why I've slowed down. His hand cradles my elbow as if he's ready to pull me back should there be any danger. I smile.

"I know what happens when the explorers are too eager to get to the treasure, and I really don't want to be in the path of blades that are about to come out of the walls or see the skeletal remains of someone with poisoned darts sticking out of their eye sockets."

Ari laughs. "I doubt you have to worry about that here. A place that has sconces to light the way and is even completely free of spiderwebs tells you something."

"Yeah, they clean up after they kill," I remark, but I look more closely just the same. He's right. Although there is hard-packed dirt beneath my feet and the walls seem to be made up of hardened clay, it's remarkably clean—no creepie crawlies, which I hate—and nothing sinister, which I guess I didn't really expect. Still. I'm not saying I'm disappointed—it's a secret passageway, after all—but a little creepiness would have been cool. Of course, the fact that the passageway is made of dirt and clay adds a strange element to it all. Who builds all the luxury found in this house just to hide an earthen corridor?

When we reach the bottom of the decline, after a few more turns, a huge wooden door looms in front of us. It's old and heavy looking, and it has been through more than one battle if the gouges and gashes are any indications. In relation to the rest of the passageway, it's the dirtiest and creepiest thing here.

"Should I knock?" I whisper.

"Why? It's part of the house."

"Yeah, but I feel like I should." My mind suddenly jumps to the woman I keep seeing around the island. *The ghost.* Could this be where she has been hiding? A shiver runs through me as I think of her entering my room and making her way to my closet while I sleep. Maybe she's stared at me for a moment, watching me drool, or maybe she's held up a knife, ready to slit my throat. I shiver again and look back the way we have come before turning to the door once more.

Ari rubs my arm and gives me a comforting smile. "We don't have to go in if you don't want to. You know where it is now, and you can come back whenever you want."

"Why don't *you* open the door, and I follow you?" I ask. This whole time, I've been the one leading, and I wonder momentarily if maybe it's a trap. Maybe this isn't such a good idea after all.

"Because this is your retreat. I'm just along for the ride."

"Yeah, but you know this place."

"Not really. Nick knows this place better than I do. I knew of its location. I knew that one day the owner would sell, but I never stepped inside until a few days ago."

"Like me? It's weird we didn't bump into each other before we did." Ari doesn't say anything, just shrugs.

I eye the passage leading back up to the closet. I could turn back. No harm done. But that would be hiding, and I'm tired of hiding. Tired of not taking chances.

I turn back to the door and heave a sigh. "Oh, fine," I say, and I turn the handle.

# Chapter 22

"Wow! Look at all this stuff!" The room is nothing like I expected; at least, not as far as the rest of the house is concerned, but I don't know if anyone was meant to find this room in the first place, so maybe it doesn't matter if it's part of the house or not. Regardless, it's a mess in a really cool treasure hunting sort of way. Not that there are gold and jewels, but there's just so much stuff that it's hard to focus on any one thing. Books are piled everywhere, along with all kinds of trinkets, gadgets, furniture, and trunks.

I want to wade through it all and could easily spend the rest of my time on the retreat just making my way down to this room to explore its contents.

"This place is just hidden away down here, and no one would think to look for it. Does the current owner even know all of this stuff is here?"

"Well, everyone accumulates stuff, and eventually they have to go through it all, right?"

I move away from the door and farther into the room. It's windowless, which is no big surprise, and twice the size of the bedroom I'm staying in.

I look at a basket. It reminds me of Mrs. Gulch—the lady Dorothy thinks of as the Wicked Witch of the West in *The Wizard of Oz*. "Huh."

"What?"

"I was just thinking of Lyn. Every year, we would watch *The Wizard of Oz*." I point to the basket, and at first, Ari looks at me blankly before understanding comes to his eyes.

"Toto," he says, smiling.

"Just once a year we'd watch," I continue. "It was tradition. We'd get on our pajamas and snuggle up under a blanket. My mom would make hot chocolate and popcorn, and we knew it was a treat because we weren't allowed to eat in the living room normally—or stay up late—and once a year . . . well, it was like we got to break the rules."

I smile, remembering. "Lyn and I were like night and day watching it. I'd sit close to my mom, almost in her lap, and I would hide my eyes whenever the Wicked Witch showed up until I was brave enough to watch. Lyn though— Lyn would watch with eyes wide open, taking everything in. It was like she wasn't afraid of anything."

I think of the grown woman Lyn is today, and although the knowledge has always been there, it hits like a bolt. "We're exactly the same as we were then," I murmur.

I rifle through some stuff on a table, a yo-yo, a box of beads, costume jewelry, and some trinket boxes before moving some blankets off the seat of a couch and sitting down. It isn't my style, unlike the couches in the house, but it's nice-looking, comfortable, and strangely free of any dust considering how long it looks as if this place has been untouched. Lyn would like this couch. It would be the type of couch she would own.

Ari sits on the couch and whatever trance I'm in is broken. I turn to him and apologize. "I don't know why I'm thinking of Lyn so much. You'd think we never see each other when I could just go back upstairs and bring her down."

Ari's brow furrows. "Wait, Lyn's here?"

I look down sheepishly. "Yeah, sorry about that. I guess I should have asked if she could come with us, but I wanted—"

"Yes?" Ari's eyes sparkle in the faint light of the room as he leans closer.

I give him a quick peck on the mouth. "I wanted to get to know you without my mirror image—"

"Mirror image?"

"—getting in the way," I finish, thinking about how awful and true that statement is. Since we're together a lot, I guess I feel pushed into the background. It's not something Lyn does on purpose, and if I'm honest with myself, I know she's not the one pushing me back. I go there willingly. I do it to myself. Sometimes I think I just want to be able to have people ask me questions, be interested in something I have to say, instead of always looking to Lyn for worthy conversation. But as I sit here, I realize I have to make the effort.

"Getting in your way, huh?" Ari's voice is soft, and he touches my cheek. The way he looks at me makes me feel vulnerable. I want to climb onto his lap, wrap my arms around him.

I sigh instead and answer his first question. "Yes, mirror image. Asymmetrically identical. What I see when looking in the mirror is what I see when I look at her. I see her, and she sees me. I'm pretty sure everyone has always been able to tell us apart though. A lot of it is our personalities. I'm surprised you haven't seen her."

"No, I haven't."

I pick invisible lint off the leg of my pants. "Good," I say.

"You don't want me to meet Lyn?"

"Yeah, of course! I mean, sure." I nod. Again, I've lost track. It's like I forget Ari is here, and yet he's the catalyst for making me think all these thoughts. "It's just . . . Lyn is . . ." I'm not sure how to continue. "I love her, but in some ways, I think I'm trying to distance myself from her—even here.

"She's always with me. I make sure she knows where I am, so if she needs me . . . all she has to do is call, but this time I *didn't* tell her where I was going, and despite that, she's right here, like always, with me."

I glance at Ari and wonder what he's thinking. Is he wishing now that he had run into the other sister? But instead of pulling away from me, he takes my hand and rubs his thumb across the skin just behind my thumb. He doesn't try to speak, doesn't try to change the subject.

"Things have been so strange since I arrived, and she said she'd stick around to be with me, and yet I keep going off by myself."

"Why do you think you're doing that?" He continues to rub his thumb across the back of my hand, and my heart melts a little. He's listening—actually listening—and he's asking me the hard questions I've been avoiding for a long time.

"Because I'm tired of feeling guilty all the time."

"Guilty for what?"

I shake my head. The things that have happened in the past are things I don't want to get into it right now, not with a guy I just met, especially after I've cleared the air with Lyn. But the thing is, I'm feeling guilty for something much more recent, something I don't want to think about. I change the subject. "And Nick has been so positive, and it's great, but I feel like he's pushing me to do something, and I don't know if I can."

Ari's voice takes on a hard edge. "Pushing you to do what?"

"That's what I'm having trouble figuring out."

I need to clear my head and stand to walk around the room, examining first one thing and then another. "Whew! That was way more than I wanted to go into. I'm sorry. I'm not trying to bore you to tears."

Ari comes over to stand near me. "I'm not bored. Why do people always think they have to make light conversation when they first meet? How do we ever really get to know each other until we start talking to each other like we're doing now?"

I laugh humorlessly. "Well, I'm not sure I know myself at this point, so forgive me if I talk in circles. I'll definitely keep you on your toes though," I end with a smile. "And it's not as if you're much of a talker," I tease.

Ari pulls me into a hug and kisses my forehead. "Do you want to get out of here and go somewhere else? We could go sit on the swing on the front porch. Or do you want to go look for other secret passageways?"

"I think I've had enough secret passageways, but thanks for showing me this one. I think I'll come back and look around some more before I leave."

We start walking toward the door. "You found it on your own," Ari says. "I just gave you a little company."

As we're about to walk out the door, I turn to take in the room one more time. I didn't see it when coming in, but now I clearly see another door on the opposite wall in a dark corner.

"Ooh, there's another door. Do you know where that one goes?"

Ari laughs. "I thought you said you were done with secret passages."

I'm already maneuvering my way around boxes and furniture to get to the far end of the room as he's talking. I grip the handle and push on the door, but it won't budge. I lean into the door, trying the handle again, but it's locked.

"This is a secret room!" I cry in disappointment. "Why lock a door in a secret room? Who *does* that?"

Ari is still standing by the door we came through, and he holds out his hand to me. "It'll open," he says with certainty as I walk back to him. "Eventually."

I reach him and grab onto his hand. "You have some insider knowledge or something?"

I swear his eyes are sad for a moment before he schools his expression. "I'm just saying, doors eventually open, right?"

My eyes sparkle with mischief as they study his for a moment. "Tell me, Ari, how do you *feel* about that?"

Ari snorts and he leans down to kiss me. "Let me tell you exactly how I feel about that," he says as we exit the room, closing the door behind us.

## Chapter 23

Shutting the secret room door and then the closet, we make our way to the closed bedroom door. I feel content, happy, like I've made a decision and I'm on a path I recently couldn't bring myself to take.

I'm telling Ari about how Gail yelled at me, wondering what his take on her reaction will be.

"So that's when I—" I gasp when I open the door to find Nick standing there, his hand raised as he's about to knock.

"Eve! I was just coming to see you."

"I can see that," I say as I glance at Ari. A huge dose of guilt courses through me, as if I've been caught with my hand in the proverbial cookie jar.

Nick sees Ari almost instantly. First, his eyes grow large, then they narrow, and he is shoving past me through the door, standing just inside my bedroom, raising a finger to Ari, and chastising him like a child.

"Why can't you just leave well enough alone?" Nick yells. His eyes are alight with an animosity I never would have thought Nick capable of, let alone with a family member.

"What are you talking about?" Ari asks, and while I'm wondering if maybe I should leave my room and let the two of them hash their differences out, he comes over to stand near me and wraps his arm around me to let me know there is no reason to be afraid. Then his arm drops, and he takes my hand.

"You always have to win, don't you, Arius?" Nick rants. "Always. You don't give a damn what you take or if it's right. You just do what you want to do, don't you?"

"It was always going to be this way," Ari says. His voice is resigned and if I have to guess, I'd say his gaze on Nick is one of pity. Mine, on the other hand, is filled with irritation. I try to yank my hand from Ari's grasp, but his fingers hold fast. The way the two are talking and glancing my way, I can tell it has to do with me. I'm a new shiny toy they both want to play with. But right now, I don't want to play with either of them.

"It doesn't *have* to be this way."

"What do you want me to do about it? It's out of my hands." Ari's fingers tighten around mine, and anger, deep and throaty, edges into his voice. He leans toward Nick as if he's about to pounce on him, and I lift my other hand to place it on his arm in case I have to try to restrain him.

"Guys," I try. "Is this really necessary?" But they continue to talk over me. It's as if I'm not even here.

"You know what you should do!" Nick shouts, his face a vivid red and his hands clenched. "For fuck's sake, don't pretend you're stupid."

"So, what—just this one time?" Ari asks. "Or does it mean I'll have to do it always? And if I do, where do I draw the line, Phoenix? Huh?" Ari is quiet for a moment as he watches his brother and allows his words to sink in. I can feel him trembling through our linked hands, and I rub my other hand up and down his arm in a show of comfort. This is more than about me. I have no idea what the hell they're talking about and feel like I should leave and allow them to carry on without an audience, but I'm trapped, not only by Ari's hand squeezing mine and Nick blocking the door, but by my curiosity.

"But it's not—" Nick's head tips back, his eyes closed. This is an argument they've had before. Both their mannerisms confirm it, and from the looks of it, it's one in which Nick has always been on the losing side.

"When have you ever been able to determine that?" Ari's words are quiet, so the roar of his next words makes me jump. "*Never*, that's when. And when you can, come talk to me." He shakes his head and his mouth trembles. When he looks at Nick, his eyes are shining with unshed tears. "Seriously, I'm begging you to, brother, because sometimes I hate it every bit as much as you do."

Nick nods tightly and for a moment, it looks like he's going to concede, but he takes in the sight of my hand clasped in Ari's and it seems to set him off. "Doesn't look like you hate it too much this time," he says, his lip curling in a sneer.

"And what the hell am I supposed to do?" Ari asks, his voice rising again. Nick's eyes catch mine and Ari's follow. With both of them staring at me, I drop my gaze to the floor and wish I could burrow into the wood like a termite.

"You want me to turn my back?" Ari continues. "You think I have a fucking choice? Do you? When some—" he pauses and glances at me— "*property* deserves to be demolished but gets a last-minute reprieve, do you rejoice? Do you see that as a win? Wake up, Phoenix. It's *always* been this way."

Nick gives an exasperated breath and runs his hands roughly through his hair. His beautiful green eyes dance between Ari and me before he turns away and paces just inside the doorway.

Ari releases his grip on my hand by degrees until it is only loosely entwined with his, and I almost whimper in relief when my nails are no longer cutting into the fingers beside them because of the pressure of his hold. I peek at his face and note the hard lines and contours I didn't see earlier. It's as if his face has aged considerably based on one conversation, one disagreement.

I wonder if I should say something, but both Ari and Nick seem to be caught up in their own thoughts. Nick walks over to the window and stares down at the lake, and Ari has gone back to rubbing the back of my hand with his thumb, his eyes on something only he can see.

"I think I should—" I start, but Nick straightens and turns from the window, walking toward the door. "Good night, Eve," he says and walks out.

"Wait!" The minute the word comes out of my mouth, I know I should have made more of an effort to keep it inside. The whole situation is tense, awkward. There is no reason I should force either of them to spend another moment in the other's company, but that's essentially what I'm doing.

"Why did you want to see me?" I sheepishly ask.

Nick looks at Ari and then back at me. "I was just going to ask you if you wanted to go out for a picnic tomorrow."

I, too, look at Ari before responding. Can things be any more awkward? As much as I've enjoyed my time with Ari, there's still a part of me that feels I owe Nick a chance too. "Um, yeah, sure," I say. "I think we need to talk." *We need to talk.* Those can be some of the worst words ever, but a grin light up Nick's face as he turns away, even as I see Ari's face darken before he pulls his hand away from me.

"See you tomorrow then," Nick says, waving as he heads to the stairs. Ari scowls and steps out of my room. He opens his mouth to say something, then closes it and shakes his head.

I don't know what to do or say, so I reach out and touch his arm. "I'm sorry," I say. I already told him I was drawn to both him and his brother, but I didn't have to do what I just did. I cringe as I anticipate a diatribe of how I broke some dating code or another by agreeing to see one guy in front of another. And if points are taken, I'm sure several will be deducted for agreeing to go for a picnic with one brother in front of another.

"It's not your fault," he says, shaking his head stonily. I can see hurt and anger in his eyes, and I'm sure most of it is directed at me.

"Did you still want to go out and sit on the swing?" I venture, expecting the rejection. Hell, I'd say no too.

216

"Yeah, ah, no," Ari says, making his excuse. "I don't think I'd be very good company."

I nod. The refusal hits harder than I thought it would. He says it wasn't my fault, but I know I had something to do with it. That was painfully obvious. I glance down the hall, wondering if I'll see Lyn peeking out her door, her eyes bright with curiosity, or see Gail and Hammond hovering off in the distance, but everything's quiet.

I don't want to have to constantly defend my actions. This was my first "date" with Ari, and just because I kissed him doesn't mean I'm ready to commit to him exclusively. At the same time, it's not exactly a *date* I'm looking for with Nick, and I'm sure there are ways I could have handled things better. If I had more dating experience, I'd probably know what those were. "I'm sorry," I repeat.

Ari leans forward and kisses my forehead. "You have nothing to apologize for. That was between me and my brother."

"Yeah, but I told him I'd go out with him right in front of you," I say because I can't keep my foot out of my mouth. "That was rude."

Ari snorts. "Didn't you hear him? He says I always win in the end." He's silent for a minute, then he touches his

217

finger to my cheek. "But Eve, this isn't a competition and you're not a prize."

I don't know whether I should take that as a compliment or an insult, and Ari must realize what it sounds like too. He laughs. "I mean, I like you. I want to get to know you, and I'll wait if I have to. If that means you have to consider your options and go out with my brother, so be it. Okay?"

I breathe a sigh of relief and throw my arms around him. My little light shines a bit brighter.

## Chapter 24

I was able to make it to the dock. I'm sitting on it now. Granted, my eyes are closed, and some could argue that I'm more on the grass right next to the dock than on the dock itself, but it's progress.

Lyn is a few feet away, on the dock itself, her legs hanging down and her toes skimming the water. It was her idea to come down here, and I'm wondering when she'll get up the courage to tell me whatever it is she wants to say. It's her MO. She usually makes herself scarce when she's considering something, so when she shows herself and asks me to come along with her for a walk or a picnic and she tries to make it seem all casual, that's when I know.

This morning, Lyn was in my room when I woke up. She was sitting on the window seat looking down at the water. When I asked her what was going on, she came over to my bed, a bounce—too much bounce—in her step and a smile too bright on her face.

"Hey you, sleep good? I mean, well." That's what she said. Another clue. She never cares about her grammar unless she is trying to make sure her setup is perfect.

Then she "confessed" that she hadn't taken a look around the island as much as she wanted to and asked me to come along and show her any of the potentially good spots she was missing out on. It was all a crock of shit. She doesn't care about the island or she'd have been all over it, most likely with a fine-toothed comb.

I could have invited her to find the door in my closet, could have seen her face when she discovered for herself the secret passage Ari and I had traversed the night before. But I didn't. It was my secret—mine and Ari's. Somehow, I didn't feel right inviting Lyn into that space with me, just as I wasn't sure if I wanted to tell her about my date with Ari—or the big blowup between him and Nick. It wasn't that I didn't think she would be supportive. I knew she would, but now more than any other time before, I felt it best to keep silent. My date and the room were mine to savor, and the thing between Nick and Ari, well, it wasn't mine to share.

So now I wait. Instead of opening my mouth to tell her about what feels like one of the most important things that has happened to me—me feeling comfortable enough with a guy to let my guard down—I keep my mouth shut and wait for her to talk to me instead, like I know she needs to.

She clears her throat. *Here we go.* Her legs still swing leisurely in the water for a moment, two. They stop swinging and she turns toward me.

"I've been thinking," Lyn starts, but she doesn't continue. I know better than to ask.

Lyn clears her throat again. "I'm ready to go back to the mainland." She props her knees up, wraps her arms around them, and rests her chin against one as she finally looks at me.

My heart starts hammering. My thoughts go to my conversation with Ari and how this is pretty much what I wanted, a chance to be on my own, to be free. So why does it feel like she's asked me to jump into the lake?

"Umm, okay," I say, hoping that's the end of it but at the same time, hoping she'll say more.

"This is something you need to do." She has a hard time meeting my eyes, and I wonder what she is not telling me.

"Why do you think that?"

"We've hardly seen each other while we've been here. Clearly, you have some things you need to figure out, and it seems like I'm just getting in the way."

And there's the guilt. "Lyn, I may have gone off on my own, but—"

"Why do you do that?"

"Do what?" I ask, the thread of my thought lost with her abrupt question.

"Why is it whenever I'm trying to get you to open up, you always believe I'm shutting you down?" Lyn kicks a wave, and a spray of droplets coat her calves. "Eve, I'm you and you're me. We've always said that, remember? I'm not going to judge you. Ever. Period. You understand? Why do you always have to think I'm out to get you?"

She wants to know? Fine. I'm willing to tell her. "You just said you felt like you were getting in the way, so that tells me you don't feel I'm paying much attention to you. I'm sorry, okay? I do have some things on my mind, and no, I don't want to talk about them."

As I'm talking, she's shaking her head, denying what I'm saying, and right when I'm about to yell at her for that because it irritates the hell out of me, she looks me in the eye.

"And that's fine. Have your space! No problem. I really don't mind. Seriously." Narrowing her eyes, she stares at me for a moment until she's sure I understand what she's saying. Sure, I understand, but simply because she says something doesn't mean she's actually feeling that way, and that's what I'm trying to determine as my own eyes bore into hers.

"This is *your* retreat, and if you don't want to talk to me—which, again, fine by me—then there's no point in me being here. I'd much rather be home."

I arch my shoulders back and hear and feel a satisfying snap. It's not enough to relieve all the tension, but it's a start.

"How come it always feels as if you're trying to make me feel guilty?" I pick up a hardened clump of dirt and hurl it into the water. Lyn scoots over until she's sitting right beside me.

"Sorry, but that's not something I do. If you're feeling guilty, it's because you feel guilty about something. What did you do? Is there something you're not telling me? Did you figure out how we got here? You dragged me onto the boat, didn't you?"

Her words trigger a flash of memory. Maybe it's the boat ride over, but I doubt it because even though I'm on a boat, I'm smiling—laughing even. I'm definitely on a boat though, and my breath quickens. "I'm not ready to face them yet."

Lyn's wearing a puzzled expression. "Huh?"

I shake my head to focus. It feels like my head is filled with cobwebs, but I don't want to clear them away. I'm not brave enough to see what's hiding behind them. "Look, having you here makes it that much harder for me to deal with whatever I have to deal with, because I think of you, and I feel guilty whenever I'm around you."

"Why?"

"I don't know." I play with a knot in the plank of wood under my fingers.

"You have to have some idea," Lyn says. She watches the water instead of me, knowing it'll help me talk as it has in the past, but this time it doesn't work. My words are fighting to rise, but a part of me doesn't want to free them.

"No, I don't know."

Lyn turns to me, skepticism written on her face. "Really?

"I don't know." There's a hard edge to my voice, and I feel like I'm going to throw up.

"Bullshit."

Anger wells inside me. Every muscle tenses, and my fingers curl into fists. If I had a bit more gumption, I'd push her in the water. "Excuse me?"

Lyn enunciates each word, so they are distinct and separate. "I. Call. Bullshit. You just said you feel guilty, so tell me why you feel fucking guilty."

"Because I let you down, okay?" I say, my voice loud and harsh in my ears. "I should have been there on the bridge. I should be there for you always—you and me, me and you. And it pisses me off because what about my life? I'm so busy being so fucking cautious all the time, and after what happened, it made me even more cautious . . . and I don't have a fucking life! Where the hell did my life go?"

Anger stings my eyes and I wipe the tears away from my face roughly with the back of my hand. "I've been too busy worrying about what could happen that I haven't"—I search for the words and snicker as it comes to me— "I haven't tested the waters."

Eleven and a half years ago, she was walking one of the trails we always used to go on. I hadn't really wanted to go. It was drizzling, and I wasn't feeling well. We had traveled the trail so many times, and others were always on the trail, so Lyn decided to go. No big deal.

The trail wasn't what anyone would call dangerous. Sure, we had to be careful not to lose our footing over some of the rough terrain, but if we did, it wasn't as if we would fall several feet or anything—or so we thought.

At one point, the trail crossed an old wooden suspension bridge that squeaked and groaned over a creek fifteen feet below.

We never had problems with the bridge and even took selfies with the creek below in the background. Everyone did. But this time was different. Lyn slipped on one of the wooden planks. That would have been okay had she not landed with all her weight on the one she landed on. According to the official report, Lyn landed on a plank with a hairline fracture—how they determined that, I have no idea—and down through it she went. But that wasn't all. Lyn's lower body went through the hole left by the broken piece of wood, but her upper body got stuck thanks to her arms.

Lyn, after calling for help and not seeing anyone on the trail, shimmied one of her arms through the hole to get to the phone in her pocket. That's when the rest of her body fell through the hole. When she landed, she fractured the tibia in her left leg, shattered the ankle of her right, and bruised a few ribs. She was found, unconscious, six hours later in the creek bed. Luckily, there were only a few inches of water, despite the rain, and her head was turned in such a way that she could still breathe without inhaling water.

Anyway, Lyn's fifteen-foot fall was halted by her body getting stuck, saving her a few feet, which the doctors say could have been the difference between life and death.

Although I knew her injuries weren't life-threatening, I remember the fear I felt. She was doing something we did all the time. She could have died. And if she had died, how could I have gone on without her?

Lyn smiles as if reading my thoughts. "Ahhh, there it is," she says.

Anger still courses through me, and I shoot her daggers with my eyes. "Want to clarify, Dr. Fucking Freud?"

"You are putting the guilt on yourself. Still. I thought we talked about this. Maybe it's because you're afraid."

"What the hell, Lyn?"

"Remember when we were little, I can't even remember how old, and we were playing in the backyard when this guy came out from between two houses out back?" Lyn smiles at her recollection, but all I feel is a shiver across the back of my neck. I do remember. It was one of the times I almost peed my pants.

"You were so afraid," Lyn continues. "Here was this stranger, and he was acting kind of weird, carrying a heavy sack, and you're tugging on my arm, trying to get me to go inside with you, your instincts shouting, 'Stranger Danger', and I was too curious. I wanted to know what the guy wanted."

I pick up the story when Lyn goes silent. "I ran inside to tell Mom. I think I was screaming. I was convinced you were about to be kidnapped, and it was up to me to make sure Mom could get to you in time to save you."

"And it turned out it was a guy from a news channel who was going around interviewing people for something or another, I can't even remember what now, and he decided to get a kid's perspective."

Despite myself, I laugh, and Lyn joins me. "Mom laid into him," I said. "His face was beet red."

"Mom made him apologize to you for scaring you so bad." Her smile fades. "Anyway, for some reason, it seems you've always felt like you had to—needed to—do everything, be better than you need to be. Does that make sense? It's like you have this . . . this need to be responsible for Every. Little. Thing. And I guess I should have told you sooner, but you don't need to. Live a little." Lyn puts her hands on my shoulders and when she looks into my eyes, it's as if she can read my soul. "You are not responsible for everything that happens. You don't get to determine how someone else feels. You are just a small, small grain of sand on a very large—"

"I get it," I say with a glare, but I also feel a knot loosening in my chest.

Lyn smiles. "Shitty things are going to happen, and you know what? That's life. So, take that burden off your shoulders, okay?"

My eyes mist over, and I pull Lyn into a hug. "I just— I don't want the people I love to be unhappy ever, not when I can do something to help. I love you, but I can't be there all the time." I whisper. There's something more I need to tell her. I keep skirting around it, going back to the accident, but it's more than that, more recent, but I'm not ready to face it, and maybe part of it is because I'm afraid she won't forgive me.

"I know," she whispers back as her arms around me tighten. "You know I love you too."

I hug her harder and blink rapidly.

We're both silent for a while, and I have enough courage to tell her at least one truth. "I like having you with me even if you're not there all the time, you know?"

"Do you want to come back with me?" Lyn asks, and I know she wants me to say yes, but I'm so tired. I want to go home too, but I just want to rest for a few days more. I smile sadly, knowing the disappointment I'm causing, even as I shake my head.

"I'll stay with you then."

"You don't—"

"Eve, it's fine. I want to. I'll be here if you need me. It's only a few days more, and there's plenty to do to keep me occupied when you don't. I offered to help Hammond and Gail with some projects they're behind on anyway."

It's exactly what I needed her to say.

We sit holding each other, and as I listen to the water slapping against the dock, I feel a weight lift off me. It's not completely gone, and I know it won't be until I get her to forgive me for everything, but I'm ready to let most of it go now, at least the burden that's been weighing down so many other aspects of my life for the last decade. Taking a deep breath, I relax, my shoulders lower than they've been for the first time in a very long time, and despite the concerns I still have, I feel a lot looser, almost free. It's a relief I never hoped to have again.

## Chapter 25

After our heart to heart yesterday, we ended up talking about Ari and Nick. I broke down and told Lyn about my night with Ari, although I didn't tell her about the room, and I told her how Nick had come by to ask me out to lunch without going into what happened before it. She didn't make any of her usual lewd comments when I talked about the kiss, and the more I think about it, she didn't really have much to say at all, which is unusual for Lyn. Instead, she seemed like she was thinking, like what I was saying was making her think of something else.

I tried asking her about it, but she just shook her head. "It sounds romantic," she said. "Keep me posted."

And that was that.

Lyn went in to help Hammond and Gail, and I enjoyed walking around the island for a while, especially since the sun was shining.

And as I walked through the prickly grass and listened to the caw of crows as they flitted from tree to tree, I reflected on the argument between Nick and Ari the night before. On some level, it had something to do with me, but there is obviously much more to it. And although it was a dumb move on my part to agree to a picnic in front of Ari, regardless of him saying he didn't mind, my sole intention was to get answers. At least, that was my objective. But when he showed up and acted as if his argument with Ari never happened, the words died on my lips. My resolve did as well. I didn't want to set him off again, and in the whole scheme of things, it's none of my business. I do wonder though.

I saw the ghost again yesterday too—inside the house. And again, she was soaking wet like she had been when I saw her by the child's bedroom. It was after Nick had left, and I had come inside to read. Storm clouds had moved in quickly, erasing the warmth and threatening a downpour, and curling up with a good book and a mug of tea sounded perfect. It's when I went to get the tea that I saw her. She was just sitting on one of the couches in the living room, and she didn't seem to care she was dripping all over it. From what I could see of her profile, her eyes were fixed on nothing in particular, and it was almost as if she was waiting for something. Having seen her so many times, I didn't feel frightened, and I went to the doorframe to talk to her.

"Are you okay?" I asked. I wasn't surprised when she didn't respond. She didn't even turn my way, although I have to think she knew I was there.

"Do you want me to get Gail or Hammond for you? Do you want me to get you a towel?" Her clothes were sticking to her, and her hair was plastered to the sides of her face. Still, she said nothing.

"I'm going to see if I can find someone, okay? I'll be right back." I ran through the rooms calling for Gail and Hammond, even for Lyn, but I couldn't find them. When I got to the library, I grabbed a throw draped over one of the chairs and ran to get back to the living room, hoping the rooms wouldn't shift on my way there. They didn't, but of course, when I got there, the ghost was gone.

I don't know why I went running for Hammond or Gail in the first place, maybe for validation. I'm the only one who has seen her, and I wonder if she's getting close to saying or indicating something to let me know who she is and why she keeps showing herself to me.

When I walked up to the couch she had been sitting on, it was pretty much as soaked as she was. But then, so was the other couch in the room. The chairs too. Everything seems to be like that now, and for that, I have no answer.

And that's been my existence for the last day and a half. A series of things that don't make sense but I'm having a hard time talking to people about. Although I've seen Hammond and Gail around the manor now and then, they always seem to be in a hurry to do something or be somewhere else, so I haven't been able to ask them if they know anything about the woman, and Nick already told me, when I brought her up before, that he didn't know who she was. As far as asking Ari . . . Well, I would ask him if I saw him around, but he's been absent since the night before last.

Today, I awoke to the sun shining through the windows, and now, I sit on the porch steps and take in the serene view. Each time I come out, I'm amazed at how quiet it is, besides the constant sound of lapping water. I expect an absence of noise inside the enormous manor, but outside, I can't help but think I'll hear the roar of a motorboat any minute or the sound of laughter and music playing on phones or portable players. Instead, I'm lulled by the whisper of the wind, the sigh of leaves, the gentle slap of the waves against the dock.

I get up and wander closer to the shore. I'm amazed at how far I've come. My fear of the water has diminished. I'm able to walk over the bridge out back without reservation, and I'm able to, at least, sit next to the dock. As I gaze out at the lake, a memory flickers. It's one I've had a few times now, where I'm on a boat—a yacht—but I don't know when it could have been.

Racking my brain does nothing to evoke more of a recollection. I've seen movies with boats and water, and they don't freak me out, but this isn't a memory of a movie. It's something that involves me—I think. But it's possible it was Lyn. . . Maybe my brain, after seeing her and Nick on the boat together our first day here, has turned it into a yacht. It's a possibility, but I doubt it's as simple as that.

I could ask Lyn, but she has been evasive since we sat on the dock together yesterday morning. I guess we both have. She's staying true to giving me time to solve my issues, and I'm taking her up on it. I just wish her whole, *"You need to figure things out"* –with emphasis on *you*— didn't include how we got here.

The approach of the sound of a motor takes me out of my reverie, and I wave as Nick pulls up with the boat and cuts the engine. Yesterday, he suggested another picnic today, but I don't see the picnic basket, and I wonder if he's going to ask me to try to go to a restaurant instead. My heart starts to pound, and the peaty smell of algae almost sets off my gag reflex until I straighten and throw my head back with determination. I can do this.

He stands in front of me, offering his hand, but we aren't headed back to the boat like I thought. No, we stop at a spot halfway under the shade of an enormous old maple tree and close enough to the lake to see the sun-worn dock and Nick's tied-up boat swaying in the sluggish current. Trees bow out over the lake, their trunks casting green reflections over the water.

We're both quiet, and my thoughts go to Ari. I haven't seen him since the night before last. I still want to ask Nick what their argument was all about; I want to ask if they were ever close, but like yesterday, we don't talk about him. We're two ostriches keeping our heads buried in the sand. Instead, we focus on what will happen when I'm no longer on the island.

"What will you do when you get back?"

"Well, the first thing I'll do is probably kiss the ground," I say with a grin.

Nick smiles too. "And after that?"

I lean back on my hands and stare out at the lake, not even a hint of fear coursing through me. "I'm not sure. I'll probably go back to work, see some friends, get back to life," I say, the knowledge of getting back into the whole routine giving me a sense of satisfaction, but a part of me also feeling as though after being here, nothing will ever be the same again.

Nick must see the realization in my face.

"Don't you want to get back to all those things? I mean, if it's not enough for you, maybe I could visit you too. I'm kind of interested to see if you'd faint on me on the mainland."

I smile. It's sweet, and I hope he does visit me. Meeting Nick and getting to know him has been like finding a brother I never knew I had, like finding a piece of myself, but I still think he may want something more than what I'm willing to give him, so I stay silent.

I lean back on my hands, close my eyes, and angle my face toward the sun's rays, soaking in its warmth. If I didn't know Nick was sitting next to me, I could imagine I'm the only person in the world, so quiet and peaceful it is. Even the harsh caw of the crows flying overhead are muted to such a degree that, had I not seen them before shutting my eyes, I would have thought their cries part of the water's wake.

"Systematic desensitization," I say, the words popping into my head.

"Huh?"

"Systematic desensitization." I open my eyes. "It's a type of behavioral therapy to get a person to not be so anxious.

That's what you're doing, isn't it? You're getting me closer and closer to the water, going to different locations so I can see it from different angles, hoping I'll eventually go in."

"No, I'm not," he says even as he begins to nod his head. He looks down at our hands and begins to caress mine with his fingers. "Ok, fine. I am. Is it working?"

I pull my hand away, smile, and stand up. "I want to show you something," I say as I proceed to walk toward the shore. Blades of grass, dry and sharp despite their proximity to water, bite into my feet and ankles and give way to more and more patches of colorful gravel the closer I am to the lake. When I get there, I stand inches from where the water can touch my toes.

"Eve! This is amazing. I'm so proud of you!" Nick stands beside me and wraps me in a one-armed hug.

Giving him a small smile, I shake my head. "I've always been able to get close to water. I take showers, you know, even baths." I look up at him sideways and smirk before turning to the greenish-blue expanse in front of me. "It's beautiful, but when I—" Breaking off, I dip my toes in the water and hiss. "When I touch a body of water outside, just touch it," I say as I move my foot back to where it's safe from getting wet, "it feels as if all of it will swallow me up and I won't be able to breathe.

"When I first got here, I thought I was going to die."

Nick's eyes dart to mine and for a second there's something I'm unable to read. "What?" he asks, concern lacing his voice.

"Not literally—okay, maybe a little literally. I saw I was surrounded by water and I couldn't understand how I got here or why I was here, and I felt like it was closing in on me." I look out across the great expanse of water, water I'm standing next to but not *in*, and some of that irrational fear returns.

I think about the small footbridge in the back of the manor and how I'm able to not only cross it but to splash in the water under it as well, and I wonder now if just thinking about my fear is making me take a huge step backward in terms of progress. The water there is clear and shallow, the bottom completely visible. Here, though, that isn't the case.

Talking has allowed me to remain calm, but I can feel beads of sweat forming on my forehead when I see Nick move so both his feet are submerged up to his ankles in the murky depths. He lifts one foot and then the other, and I can clearly see he is intact, that nothing awful is happening, but it doesn't stop me from leaning forward, grabbing his hand, and pulling him out and away from the water's edge, my heart hammering in my chest.

Nick pulls me in for a hug, and I cling to him for moments before relaxing my grip. He looks down at me, but I can't identify the expression that flashes on his face before he places a kiss on my forehead. "I'm sorry, Eve," he says. It sounds so foreboding. Giving me a small smile, he points to the boat. "I'll go get the picnic basket."

## Chapter 26

"**S**o, how much longer do you think we'll be here?" Lyn whines. She's draped over a chair in an office I decided to peek in. There's not much here besides filing cabinets, which I'm not *so* nosey to peek into, a couple of comfy chairs, and a massive desk, but I wanted to take a look just the same.

I know she's eager to get going. I'm feeling the same. It hasn't been much of a retreat since I seem to be waiting for something to happen more than being able to relax.

"Tomorrow's our last full day here," I say. I really am curious how I'll leave. I know Nick wants me to leave under my own steam, but if I faint again, they're going to have to take me like that. Lakeview Manor is wonderful, but I can't live here indefinitely. "I keep waiting for Gail to ask if our bags are packed, but I haven't seen her or Hammond since yesterday."

"For two people who always seem so busy all the time, how come the house looks more rundown now than it did when we came here? If we threw huge parties, sure, but you, my dear girl, are no partier."

I give her a saccharine smile, but she's right. Each day, I've noticed a steady decline in the house's upkeep. More and more dust and grime accumulate, and the stench of mildew is now so powerful that the smell of the lake which I never really liked, per se, has taken on a sweet aroma, and everything seems to be wet. I don't even sit on the couches in any of the rooms anymore, choosing to sit on the more impenetrable faux-leather chairs.

"You can always ask Nick," Lyn says while looking at me sideways. "You've been seeing him quite a bit."

I give her another overly sweet smile. Again, she's right even though she's been who knows where, and I'm surprised she's current with what's been going on. Nick has been by every day, and although I really enjoy his company, I still want to see Ari again. I don't know if it's the whole idea of the one who got away or if it's something more, and I want to find out.

"If you're thinking about Ari," Lyn starts, reading my mind, "what's the point? We've only got one more day here."

"Yup." My voice is glum. I knew he affected me, but I didn't realize it was this much.

"Eve, if you're meant to see him again someday, you'll see him, but you're not going to try to stay just to see him again, are you?"

"No, I'm not going to stay here just to see him! I'm waiting to see if I'll figure all this crap out—how we got here, who that ghost woman is, why I went out the side door and landed on the porch—which hasn't happened again, by the way—and I'm also wondering how the hell I'm supposed to get back off the island."

"God, Eve," Lyn sighs as she stands, "I hope you figure it out soon. One day to be exact." She's about to walk out the door when Nick steps in the doorway.

"There you are! I've been looking all over for you!"

"Hey, Nick. Bye, Nick," Lyn says, and she pats him on the shoulder as she heads out.

Nick turns around in a circle and then lifts his hands, palms up. "Did I do something wrong?"

I smile at him. "Hi, Nick. Don't worry about her. She's getting impatient to leave." I get up from the chair, walk around the desk, and give him a hug. Nick leans back and lifts my chin with his finger so I'm looking into those exquisitely green eyes, and I can feel my face heat a little. But it's not the same pull I feel when I'm with Ari, not even close . . .

If it weren't for Ari, I wonder if I would have encouraged Nick more. He's definitely handsome. He's kind, and he's been there for me, and now that I see him again, I realize how much I miss our banter when he's not around. I push thoughts of Ari away and focus on Nick, who is now juggling pens he has taken off the desk.

"I haven't seen you since yesterday. I thought maybe you drowned." I give him a grin, but Nick pales and drops the pens. He pulls at the collar of his shirt as if it's suddenly too tight and looks everywhere but at me.

I frown. I'm the one afraid of water. Is he worried I'm going to suddenly fall apart? I'm the one who made the joke! "I was kidding, Nick. Haha." I raise my eyebrows. "What's gotten into you?"

Nick picks up the pens, hastily putting them on the desk, and two roll toward the edge. Grabbing them quickly, he lifts his head. "Actually, I'm here to give you another shot at winning my heart."

"What?" I laugh. Apparently, I read the situation wrong.

"Well, you may think playing a damsel in distress is the way to go about getting the affection of a guy, but I'm here to tell you, it doesn't work."

I narrow my eyes and tilt my head, unsure where this conversation is going. "I seem to recall you being really concerned. You mean that was just an act, too?"

"You liked that, huh? A pat on the shoulder here, a look of understanding there. It's all in the manual."

Openly grinning, I look down at the desk and then back at Nick. "Oh, really?" And right about now, I'm wondering what it would be like to have his lips on mine. I don't want to think about Ari anymore, and I want to feel something other than this overwhelming sense of waiting. Would I be taking advantage of Nick if I give in to that desire? I know it's not right, but at this particular moment, I don't care. *See, Lyn, I can be spontaneous.* "So," I say as I walk over to him, "do you think you've won my heart?"

"Let's see." Nick pretends to search my eyes. "Hmmm, oh yes, I can see allowing you to cling to my biceps was a big draw," he says as he flexes his muscles. I struggle not to laugh outright and manage to keep it to a squeak. It's not that I consider Nick scrawny by any means, but his athletic build isn't . . . Ari's.

Nick glares at me for a second and I try to look contrite. "You obviously appreciate my good looks and outstanding taste," he says, daring me to contradict with a debonair wave at his figure. "I make a mean picnic, and—" He puffs out his chest. "Of course, there's my humility." He nods with satisfaction. "It'll be a piece of cake."

"Uh-huh. And what, pray tell, would I have to do to win your heart, Mr. Anker?" I run my fingers up his tie and flick imaginary dust away. I'm hands-down, unabashedly and without hesitation flirting, and it feels great! I've missed this.

"You could . . . let me kiss you." And before I have time to think, his lips are against mine, warm and soft, and I'm kissing him back. His hands come up on either side of my face and he tilts my head, allowing him to deepen the kiss. I can't help it; I sigh and relax in his arms. It's a comfortable kiss, lazy and . . . it's not at all what I want. And it's horrible because Nick is amazing, and I know I want him in my life. But not like this. The kiss isn't filled with the passion I was hoping for. I wish it were there, but my thoughts wander yet again to Ari, and I pull away. Nick leans his forehead against mine and sighs.

"Let me take you to lunch on the mainland."

I move away from him and cross my arms. "I seem to recall that didn't go over too well the last time we tried it."

"And you said you wanted to try again."

True.

"And that's why I brought this!" Nick puts his hand in his pocket and pulls out a length of dark fabric. "A blindfold." He holds the fabric out to me and then runs it through his fingers as if it's on display. "And we can always use it later for other things," he whispers, raising his eyebrows suggestively.

Laughing, I push him away. "You haven't won my heart yet, Romeo!"

"Did you just snort?" he asks in disbelief. "I swear I just heard you snort!" He looks around the room, nodding as if there is an audience agreeing with him. "Young lady," he begins in mock horror, "a woman who snorts is no woman!" He storms out of the room and I'm laughing so hard, I'm nearly doubled over. Tears are streaming down my face, and all I can think about is how good this feels. He may not be Ari, but I could get used to this. I could.

When my hoots have succumbed to deep intakes of breath and the occasional giggle, Nick's head and shoulders appear around the door frame.

"Seriously though, you want to try it?" he asks, holding out the fabric.

I grab it and walk around him. "Ooo, I can't wait to be blindfolded," I say as I wrinkle my nose, and when I see his eyes light up and his mouth open, I quickly add, "to go to lunch."

Nick shuts his mouth and smirks. "You're learning, kid," he says. "Let's go."

We don't get past the front porch.

Heavy gray clouds greet us, and a flash of lightning seems to strike right next to the dock and Nick's boat. I flinch at the accompanying boom of thunder that rattles the windows and makes the porch vibrate.

"I don't have an umbrella," I say dumbly, but I'm not looking at the sky. I'm looking at the lake and how it has become a churning mass of angry liquid. Waves slap and beat against the boat, making it jump up and down.

"Neither do I," I hear Nick respond. "We could make a run for it," he suggests as we both look out from under the roof that barely shields us. The wind lashes at the house, causing it to shudder and shake, and the rain which a moment ago was only a slight drizzle, is now a downpour, seeking the wind's aid to sodden everything within sight, including us. The waterspouts on either side of the porch pour water, and a pool of dirty rainwater has formed at the bottom of the steps.

"Let's see if it lets up. It can't go on like this," I suggest instead. He moves us back so that we're standing against the front door. We could go inside and wait it out, but we just stand there looking at the sky, looking at the lake, looking at anything else but each other. I think he knows we're not going to be going anywhere. Even if I make it onto the dock, there's no way I'll get on a boat that appears as though it's being tossed like a child's toy in a bathtub.

"You want to go inside and have a sandwich?" I invite, my hand moving toward the doorknob. "Or maybe I can find a can of soup or something."

Nick looks at me sullenly and then returns his gaze to the phenomenon in front of us. "No." After a few minutes, he asks, "Why do you listen to him?"

"What do you mean, why do I listen to him?" I ask, trying to imitate Nick's voice. He's not amused. "Listen to who?"

"Ari. What did you two talk about in your room? Were you even talking? Did you kiss him like you just kissed me?"

I sigh. I thought it would come earlier, this questioning. Then, I hoped maybe Nick was trying to sweep it under the rug like I was. Ari was right though; the truth will come out. "Yes, I kissed him," I say, getting it out in the open. "But mainly, we talked—*I* talked. He barely said a word. He was listening to me while I was trying to make sense of everything that's going on in my head."

I stare at Nick, but he's not giving me any indication of what he's thinking. "I'm a grown adult, Nick, and you know what? I don't even know why I have to explain myself to you.

Whatever this is, it's between you and Ari. He's not a bad guy. What happened between you two to make you hate him so much?"

Nick kicks out at the rain, doing nothing but getting his shoe and pant leg wet, and mumbles something beneath his breath. "It's not about me. Hell, it's not about him either. Eve, this is about you! Can't you see that? This is your life we're talking about!"

No longer caring if I get wet, my attention is fully on Nick. "What the fuck, Nick? Seriously. What the hell are you talking about, and why do you even care? You've known me, what, not even a week now? And suddenly you know what's best for me and my life? Do you even know anything about my life? You have some stock in it I don't know about or something?"

Nick snorts and walks a few feet away from me to the edge of the first step on the porch. The rain is beating down on him, but he doesn't seem to care. It looks like he's going to leave, but he stops. I watch as his back lifts and lowers, his breathing quick. His hands clench into fists. He stands like this for minutes, and I . . . I feel sorry for him. He's struggling with something I don't understand. For a moment, I feel united with him. I'm struggling too. When he speaks, his voice is strained but controlled.

"Eve, you need to figure out what you want. I'm trying to help you sort out your fears, but I can only do—"

"What were you and Ari fighting about the other day?" I ask. "What were you two so worked up about—why do you two hate each other?" Ari's been gone for days and Nick still isn't happy.

"It doesn't matter," he says, his gaze lost to the rain. "Will you just . . . can you think about what I said? Please? Think about who has your best interest at heart, okay?"

My hands clench into fists, tired of half-ass answers and riddles. "Do I look like a child to you?" I ask, my voice calm despite my mounting irritation. Nick's eyes widen, but he shakes his head. "Someone who can't make up my own mind?" Again, he shakes his head. "Someone who doesn't fucking *think* about the consequences of her own actions? That's all I've been doing since I've been here is *thinking*."

Nick's shaking his head vigorously now, and he opens his mouth to contradict, but my hand comes up to ward off further words and still his tongue. "How dare you assume anything about my life when you don't know me at all."

Nick's eyes flare and he stomps over to me "I don't know you?" He shakes his head in disbelief. "I don't know you?" he repeats, his eyes widening. "I know that you hide behind Lyn every chance you get because you're afraid of letting people see the real you. I know you're afraid to let life in because of any potential hurt that might come with it, that you worry about letting the people you love down, that you feel you care too much." He almost growls as he rakes his fingers through his hair. "And I know there's something that scares you more than the water down there—" He points to the lake. "And that's the truth about what's going on in here," he says, stabbing his finger at the air around my head.

My heart is beating triple-time and my breaths are short, almost panting. How could he know . . . ? But that could be anyone. It doesn't make his words any less true. He watches as I process, my emotions surging from indignant incredulity to suspicion to almost unfounded grief and resignation. Tears well in my eyes and I shake my head, wanting to tell him he's wrong but knowing he's right. "Why are you doing this?" I ask, my voice a whisper. "Why are you saying these things?"

Nick studies the sky still pouring rain and then the lake, still a churning torrent of swells. Finally, he looks at me. "When I first saw you, it was like there was this light. You exuded it. But the light has faded." I open my mouth to interrupt, but he holds his hand up this time to stop me. "I blame Ari."

"But I haven't even seen him since the other night," I say, shaking my head.

"You kissed him," he says simply. "I don't know what else to say, Eve. Maybe I'm jealous." He gives me a small, sad smile. "I don't want him to steal my sunshine."

And like almost every girl who has seen a guy say something absurdly cheesy in a romantic movie, I melt—just a little. What is it with these two and their corny phrases, and why am I such a sucker for them?

We continue to wait out the storm. The lightning appears less and less frequently, the rolls of thunder sound more and more distant until all that's left is a gentle patter as droplets hit the foliage of nearby trees. The water, dark and muddy, calms as well until the familiar lap replaces the ruthless turbulence.

I step out from beneath the eaves, and the rain starts back up in earnest. Each drop seems to hit me with precision, and before I can even step back to the relative safety of the eaves, my clothes are damp and rain drips from my hair. There's a coolness in the air that makes me shiver, and I turn to Nick. Before I can even open my mouth to say anything, his lips are on mine, hard, bruising, and his hands, although cupping the sides of my face, almost feel vice-like.

"Why don't you want this?" he demands, almost desperately, as he leans his forehead against mine. I'm too stunned to respond. Confusion overwhelms me, and although

I should be thinking of his kiss, it's Ari's my thoughts return to. I can feel my mouth working to say something, anything, but there are no words.

Nick steps away. There's a hardness around his eyes I've never seen before, save with Ari, and I'm about to demand he tell me what the hell is going on, but before I can open my mouth, he mumbles, "That's it then," and is striding off the porch and toward the dock.

"Nick?" He keeps his back to me, not bothering to answer, his long legs traversing the length of the yard in moments. Bewildered, I watch as he jumps into the boat, starts up the motor, and steers away from the dock. I will him to turn around, to say something else, but he doesn't. He doesn't even give a backward glance.

## Chapter 27

How can gray be vibrant? It's the dullest color in the world, but right now, it's the only color that seems to be highlighted. The green of the grass is tinged with it; the immense sky shows no hint of any other hue. The wood of the steps on which I sit is possessed with an overpowering impression of it. And even Nick's mood as he stomped away was filled with it.

I stare out across the gray water, watch the gray waves ripple in starts and stops as it tries to decide if it should calm or continue its agitation in the storm's wake, and think gray thoughts.

I was under the impression that retreats were quiet, restful. I was wrong. Instead, it seems I'm bombarded with thoughts of Lyn, the ghost woman, Ari, Nick . . . My mind was more at peace when I was home than it has been since I've been here.

Nick's kiss, *kisses* . . . I can't get over how different they both were. The first was so natural, so comfortable, even enjoyable. It was like participating in an activity I've always found pleasurable. I could have continued with it, but . . . *But*. And that's the thing—there was a but. With Ari, there was no but. With Ari, all my buts went out the window. Buts don't exist and if they do, it doesn't matter because I'm where I'm meant to be, and—*and*, not but—that's not with Nick.

Then the second kiss. What was that? Why was he so angry? Well, that was on me. I know I shouldn't have toyed with his emotions in the first place. I suspected he felt more toward me, and just because I haven't seen Ari doesn't give me the right to take out my aggression on Nick. I play with a splinter in the wood, and I wince at my foolishness. He had every right to be angry with me.

But the whole thing with having my best interests at heart? It had to be a part of his anger. Does he honestly think I *don't* have my best interests at heart? I've only ever had everyone's best interest at heart. That's who I am. And I've also been known to follow my conscience without needing a man—Nick or Ari—to tell me the appropriate action to take!

I pound my fist on the steps and then inhale sharply when pain radiates up my arm. In some ways, the pain dulls my frustration, so I do it again, and then once more for good measure. I'm glad he's gone. I'm glad he left in a huff. I hope he doesn't come back, and then I don't have to deal with his attitude anymore.

And I know I'm kidding myself. It hurts that he walked away so angry, that his eyes were so hard and that I was the reason. I don't like life lessons like this, the ones that hold up a mirror and force me to see something I know I need to change. I owe Nick an apology.

Do retreats turn you into self-proclaimed psychologists? I'm starting to wonder.

I listen to the soft waves as they slap against the dock, undulate, and repeat their aggression. I'm like the dock. And I wonder how many slaps I'll need before I buckle and let the waves of truth wash over me. I need answers, not to waste my time practically hyperventilating over a guy I just met. Things are bound to change once I leave the island anyway. I'll go back to my job, my life. I won't have as much time as I do now. Chances are, I'll think so much about what I'm supposed to do that I won't think about what I want to do or who I want to spend time with. I'll fall back into my old routine, stuck in a rut, afraid to get out there . . . I wonder if Nick knew how true his words were.

A noise behind me has me sitting up straighter. It's most likely Lyn coming to check up on me, and I don't want her seeing how upset I am. It's not that I don't think she could help, it's just that I'm tired of not being composed around her, and so far on this retreat, we've had more than enough heart-to-hearts where I'm the one in need of comfort.

The door opens and closes, and I take a deep breath. "I hope you're not looking for Nick because he left a little while ago, and I have no clue when he's planning on coming back. Unless you talk—" I stop when I see it's not Lyn at all.

It's Ari.

"Hi," he says, coming to stand next to me. We're both silent as we watch the occasional raindrop dance upon the lake. All the words I want to say are stuck at the back of my throat. I don't even know what they are exactly. There are too many thoughts jumbled in my head. So, I stare into the grayness. Do I tell him I kissed Nick? The first time, I essentially threw myself at him. When I was with him, it felt important to do. I needed it, but now, I don't even remember the point. I know I had one, but it's all a tangled mess, especially with how things ended.

Slowly Ari sinks to sit beside me. He reaches out his hand tentatively, and when I touch it with mine, he grasps my fingers and squeezes. I squeeze back.

"Do you want to go explore the hidden room some more?"

And because the blue of his eyes is the first color I've seen in I don't know how long, and because his hand is warm, and his proximity is intoxicating, and because he's Ari, I say yes.

➤ The House on the Lake

## Chapter 28

"So, I want to apologize . . ."

Although he holds my hand the whole way, we move silently through the house, up the stairs, through my room and closet to get to the secret passage. Letting go of my hand to undo the latch to the passage and opening the door, Ari asks if I'm all right. I nod. I am not trying to show an attitude, but I wonder if that's the way it comes across. He rakes his hand through his hair and mumbles something I can't hear before reaching out his hand again for mine. We don't say another word until we are both seated on the couch. And the first thing he wants to say is sorry?

"For what?"

"Well, I haven't seen you for a couple of days and the last time I did, I was fighting with my brother. Not exactly how I wanted our date to end, you know?" He avoids my eyes as he talks as though he's afraid to see anger or hurt. I'm glad he's not looking because he'd see guilt instead.

"I thought you were mad at me for agreeing to go out to lunch with Nick. It would serve me right. That was pretty shitty of me."

"Don't beat yourself up about it." I'm not sure what he means, and he must see my confusion because he clarifies. "I'm not into sharing if that's what you're thinking, but I understand you wanting to keep your options open." He sobers a little. "I know my brother has a certain appeal; it's one reason we're always at odds—it's always been that way with us. It's always felt like we're pitted against one another. Besides," he continues, grinning, "I like to think we had a pretty nice time, but I'm not about to stand in your way if there's something else you want. We'd both end up regretting it in the end, and I'm—well, I'm your endgame."

I laugh, waiting for a joke. "You sound pretty confident about that."

Although he smiles, it doesn't reach his eyes, which appear sad, apologetic. "I swear—and this is going to sound even cheesier than my pickup lines—I swear I will always be there for you."

I shift uncomfortably. The dedication, though sweet, is way too soon. I hardly know Ari, so to hear him state some unwavering commitment to be by my side sounds more than a little stalkerish.

Ari gets up and starts pacing the room. "Look, there are a lot of things I wish I could tell you right now, but I can't. The last thing I want to do is scare you, so just let me say one last thing and then we can drop it, okay?"

He waits for me to nod before he continues. "You may decide to choose Nick or some other guy, and that's fine—I mean, I won't like it, but it's your choice, and I get it—but regardless of that, I just want you to know I'm here for you."

I wait for a good minute to make sure he's not going to say something else. I'm not sure how to feel. I've never had a guy say anything like that to me, and it's really sweet. In some ways, I like it a lot. But it's scary too. Creepy. We've spent a few hours together. How could he possibly feel that way? Disappointment courses through me and the bitch in my head is telling me, *I told you so*. Here, I thought I had maybe stumbled upon a potential keeper, and he turns out to be unbalanced.

"I kissed Nick." I might as well tell him. Let's see if he really means what he says or if he's playing some sort of game.

Ari swallows, and I can see his jaw work as he clenches his teeth a few times. He paces the room—again. He's like a tiger in a cage, and I can't tell if I should say something else or let him finish digesting that little morsel first.

He comes back over and sits back down. "Did you have a good time?"

"Huh?"

"With Nick—did you have a good time?"

I hesitate, staring. Did he not just hear what I told him?

"Yes, yes, I heard you," he snaps, his brows drawn together. "I'd rather not think about it if you don't mind, so just tell me, since you've obviously seen him more in the last couple of days than you've seen me, did you have a good time?" Before I can answer, he snorts. "Most likely you did, or you wouldn't have kissed him, but I'm trying to be polite here, so . . ."

"It was . . . interesting."

Ari raises his head, his eyes narrowing. "How do you mean?"

"Well, first he was all friendly and flirty, and then it was raining, so we couldn't even attempt to take the boat, and when the rain started to let up, he—well, it's my fault, really. I didn't mean to hurt him, but I think I did, and he didn't take it very well and left."

Ari grabs my hand, rubbing just behind my thumb as he's done before. He lets out a breath and dips his head as if coming to some conclusion. "You didn't do anything. Nick's just . . . He has a right to be upset, but he's not upset with you. It's—it's this house." He pauses, and I can tell he's choosing his words carefully. "He's under a lot of pressure right now. The owner is having a hard time. She doesn't want to close the house, but unmitigated circumstances are pushing her to do so. Nick is holding out hope those circumstances will change. He's very passionate about the owners of our houses. He only wants the best for them, and sometimes, he gets riled up."

"Why didn't he just tell me that? Instead, he acted like it was my fault it was raining and left in a huff." I shake my head in bewilderment. "Whatever. You know, I'm here for a retreat that pretty much ends tomorrow. I'm not supposed to get involved with anyone, let alone two brothers. Perhaps it's best if we just—"

"Eve, no." Ari cuts me off and grabs my other hand so that both are trapped within his. "Please. I'm sorry I freaked you out earlier with what I said. I'd take it back if I could. There's just something about you . . . but I swear I'm not a stalker."

His eyes are pleading with mine, and I can hear the sincerity in his voice. I had a great time with him the other night, and he's funny and cute, and his voice . . . Plus, I feel like I can tell him anything. Am I going to let one little thing he said ruin something I feel in my bones will be really good?

"And as far as the kiss with Nick . . ." He pauses and my stomach clenches. He shakes his head. "I don't care." I meet his gaze and his eyes crinkle at the corners. "Of course, I *care*, but this is new, and for all I know, you didn't know if you'd ever see me again with the way I left the other night. And—let's just see where this goes, okay?"

"Okay," I say hesitantly. "Just, lay off the mozzarella, all right? I mean, all that stuff was really sweet, but you hardly know me, so for you to talk that way, it's just really—"

Ari grins, raises my hands to his lips, and kisses them one at a time. "No cheese from now on, I swear," he says, "but if you tell me to get rid of the bacon, I'm out of here."

"Ha! Well, bacon. No one in their right mind would dare!" I say in return, and I'm happy. I've hit a relationship milestone. I don't think I've ever had an important conversation like this with a guy before. But then, I guess I've never truly been in a relationship before, not really. There have been a few guys it has been nice to hang out with, fool around with, but they all fizzled out. Either I didn't return a call or plans had to be changed and rescheduling never happened . . . I never felt invested though, so the endings didn't hurt.

The ending here has the potential to hurt. I can already feel it, so the intensity of his words, well, it's not a red flag; at least, I'm hoping it isn't because even though I'm not sure if I'm ready for all that feeling, it sure would be nice to be.

"Anyway, what have you been doing for the last couple of days?" Ari says, changing the topic. "I'm sorry I haven't had a chance to see you. I would have left a message with Gail and Hammond, but I think they're avoiding me. I haven't seen them either."

"Where do you stay anyway?" I ask, ignoring his question. "You never come or go in a boat, but I've hardly seen you in the house, and with the amount of wandering I do, I'd think our paths would cross more than they have, or I would have come across your room or something."

"You want to see my room?" Ari asks, quirking an eyebrow, his azure eyes blazing.

"That's not what I meant!" I can feel my cheeks burning under his stare, and my core temperature rises from the huskiness of his voice. I want to say, *Yes, let's go now!* But the damn opinions of my inner voice, weak as they may be, are enough to have me rein myself in, tread with caution, and answer his original question. "I haven't been doing too much. I think that's kind of the point of a retreat, right?" I smile. "I've been relaxing, wandering, walking around the island when it's not raining, talking to Lyn—and did you know there's a ghost on the island?"

"What?"

"I swear. I didn't tell you before because I didn't want you to think I was crazy—"

"You're okay with me thinking you're crazy now though?"

I nudge him with my shoulder and smile. "I'm okay with you seeing how I process the world around me," I say. "There's a difference. Anyway, she has to be a ghost. At first, I thought it was Lyn because I've never seen the ghost straight on, but from the back, she looks like Lyn, but she doesn't have the same walk."

"Okay, so you've seen a person who looks like Lyn. What makes you think she's a ghost?"

I tell him about all my experiences with the ghost so far and about how each time she disappears. "Cool, right? She's kind of creepy too."

"They say ghosts are around because they're trying to give someone a message. Has Lyn seen the ghost?"

"No. Just me. I even asked Gail and Hammond about it, and *they* looked at me like I was crazy—"

"And you're sure you're not crazy? I mean, processing the world," he says, using air quotes "completely randomly from everyone around you?" He regards me with a raised eyebrow but otherwise straight face. For a moment, I think he's serious until he cracks a smile. "I'm kidding. It does sound cool. There are lots of weird things in this world. Who's to say ghosts exist or not? But as I told you before, I'm a skeptic. She clearly wants you to see her, so when you do, keep on following her. Sounds like she wants to tell you something but isn't ready to do so yet."

"You think she'll give me some message to pass on to her loved ones or something?" I ask eagerly. I'm almost tempted to go ghost hunting right now.

"You never know. But whatever it is, I would say she thinks it's pretty important." Ari opens his mouth to say more but closes it instead.

"What?"

"Well, I was just going to say that it's weird you think the ghost looks like Lyn. You said you guys are mirror twins, right? So, if she looks like Lyn, she looks like you."

"Yeah. Huh. I know it's obvious, but I don't really think of it like that. Lyn and I look alike, but we're so different." I smile. "She's like my alter ego, and I'm her conscience. I guess you're right though. Nick said something about it too."

"You think there might be a reason you're thinking so much about her?"

"I'm not. Not really. I mean, she's Lyn. We do everything together, so of course, she's going to be in my thoughts."

"It still sounds strange to me that this ghost takes on the appearance of you both. I would think that would be something I'd look into."

I turn an assessing gaze to Ari. He sounds like a therapist or my dad when he knows something I should know but haven't figured out yet. "It's something I'll consider, not that I have much time left here." An amusing thought pops into my head and I lean forward and whisper, "Maybe she's some long-lost relative, and she's trying to help me uncover some family secret, and then the house will be mine." I attempt a sinister laugh.

Instead of laughing with me, Ari looks at me pensively and nods, crossing his legs at the ankle.

"You were supposed to at least snicker."

"Maybe you're onto something." My face scrunches in disbelief at Ari's words. "Hear me out. Think about it. You arrive here and don't know how. No one has seen this ghost except for you. She looks like you. There's not a small part of you that thinks that maybe, just maybe, she's here to give you a message?"

"Then why doesn't she give me the friggin' message already? I've been here almost a week, and all this time, it's like I've been waiting for the other shoe to drop, for something to happen. Lyn knows something but won't tell me because she's waiting for me to figure it out. Nick's acting weird, so I have to figure *that* out. Now you're telling me—as a *skeptic*—that it's possible this ghost is waiting to tell me some big dark secret. Come on, seriously?"

"Seriously."

I don't want to think about it anymore, so I do something stupid. I kiss Ari. It's not like I want to kiss him. I mean, I do, but right now he's pissing me off because everything he's saying just reminds me how much I don't know, how much I don't think I want to know. I realize I'm going to have to face whatever it is I'm afraid of and recognize that time is coming soon, but I don't want it to be now. I just want to live in the moment, take what I can get, and worry about what's to come later.

At first, he does nothing; it's like I'm kissing a brick wall, but soon his lips are responding to mine, and his hand cradles my head, pulling me closer, deepening our kiss. I've almost forgotten my worries when he pulls away and searches my eyes.

"Just—you have to confront whatever is bothering you, okay? Isn't that the reason you're here?"

"No, actually. It's not. I just came to check out the house. Seriously, what is it with you and your brother? What do you know about my life?" I push away from him and slide over until I feel the arm of the couch on my back. It's not what he's saying because he's right—I do need to find answers. There's too much I don't remember—but it's more the *way* he's saying it, like it's time-sensitive or something, and he's reminding me I have a deadline. This retreat isn't going to last forever. And I'm not good with deadlines, not on the mainland, and apparently not here.

"You both act all possessive, telling me what to do or acting as if you know what's best for me or something." I jump off the couch and stomp toward the door. I'm acting like a child. I'm embarrassed and upset, and I'm angry with myself for letting Ari's concern make me feel as if I'm not working hard enough to figure my shit out. *Why am I not working hard enough?*

"I'll figure it out on my own time," I mumble over my shoulder. I turn to yank the door shut, wanting a satisfying slam, needing the noise to center me, but the sound doesn't register. My mind just holds the mental image of Ari's face right before the door bangs closed. It's full of sadness and perhaps a bit of pity too.

➤ The House on the Lake

## Chapter 29

It's too much. My mind is on overdrive now, and all I want to do is get out of here and go back to civilization. I want to get away from secret rooms and brothers and endless water. *I am going crazy; I'm having a mental breakdown. No wonder I don't remember how I got here.* That must be what it is because nothing else makes sense.

My mind racing, I slowly make my way toward the water.

Instead of going to the water's edge, I walk to the dock. I was able to walk on it with Nick's help, and I wonder if I can do it on my own. If I push myself, maybe I'll be able to actually make it to the boat next time, maybe even onto the boat and away from here.

At the dock's edge, I tentatively lift my foot. The worst that could happen is I'll faint again. I've already been on the bridge out back. I've already touched the water. I'm pumping myself up with reminders because I need this. I put my foot down and take a deep breath. I glance back to the house, stretch my neck, and then look back out upon the water. The flash of a boat enters my mind again, and my heart thumps erratically. *What the hell?*

My eyes may be on the water, but I'm searching through my memories. It's a memory I've had before, but I get an even sharper mental image. It's a yacht. It can easily fit twenty to thirty people on it, and there's a celebration. I can't see individual faces. Instead, it's like I'm hovering just over their heads. Foreheads and hats, wisps of hair blowing in the breeze, a tangy brine smell, laughter . . . No matter how hard I try, I can't get anything else.

I look down at where my feet barely touch the dock. I've been procrastinating, and I'm not even doing it on purpose. I lift my right foot again and set it on the dock. My stomach drops, but I refuse to lift my foot. Instead, I lift my left foot and place it firmly on the dock.

*Another flash of the yacht, only this time, Mr. Belcher, my boss, is there too. The hull slices through the water as crew members dressed in white suits speak soundlessly to each other and guests onboard. The railings of the polished wooden decks gleam in the overhead sun, and white lounge chairs, the ones with bright blue cushions, sit in the shade of retractable awnings. Mr. Belcher stands smiling, his sunglasses sliding down his nose in the heat.*

My breathing is ragged, and I can feel sweat dripping down my back even though I'm freezing. I try to take another step forward, but it's as if my feet are glued to the dock. I can't do anything except watch and listen, the scene playing out on the lids of my closed eyes.

*The waves crash against the hull as the boat speeds toward an unknown destination, and as I inhale lemon-scented wood polish, sunscreen, and the distinct odor of fish in the ocean air, I feel the spray of salty water and summer heat on my face.*

I'm jerked out of my reverie by the sound of thunder overhead. The contrast of the overcast sky with that of my vision is striking, and I shiver as a gust of wind pushes me back. Like a spell being broken, I'm finally able to move, and I back up off the dock, stumbling as I encounter the edge. Lightning flashes overhead and I finally tear my eyes away from the lake to glance up at the darkening sky, angry storm clouds rushing in to spit out their irritation. Only then do I find the strength to turn around and head back inside.

Where's Lyn? I search the house, the rooms graciously maintaining their positions, but there are too many of them. I call out for her; I even go up to the attic although I know she didn't like it up there, but I can't find her anywhere. My mind creates different scenarios. Maybe she got stuck outside. No, it's not like the island is so big she'd have to hide out to wait for the storm to finish. Maybe she found a secret room of her own.

Then I wonder if maybe she left with Nick. Maybe Nick came back and picked her up. I was in the room with Ari, so she wouldn't have known where I was even if she had come looking for me. Panic wells within me, as does an unshakable fear that she's left me alone. It's irrational, silly even. I told her it was okay if she did. *Please don't leave me alone.* I search for any note she might have left me instead, and when I find none, I throw my hands up. That's how Gail finds me.

Harried, she asks me if I need anything as she flits around the room, making sure buckets are in place to catch several drips of water dropping from the ceiling. I didn't even notice them before.

"Have you seen Lyn?"

"Lyn?" Gail stops what she's doing to turn to me.

"Lyn. Lyn! The one who looks like me?" My eyes widen as Gail regards me with furrowed brows. "You know, highly irregular and all that?" I demand.

"Lyn's not here," Gail says as she shakes her head. Her statement almost sounds like a question.

"Well, where is she? Did she go with Nick?"

Gail continues to shake her head. "Lyn's not here," she repeats before her eyes spring wide open. "Oh!" she says,

"Oh dear, oh dear, oh dear." She practically runs out of the room, and I don't know if she heard something I didn't or if she's just trying to avoid talking to me any longer.

"Argh!" I shout, deciding to go outside. Maybe Nick will come back soon, and I can ask him to take me off this island once and for all. I don't care if he has to hogtie me to get me on the boat and away from here. I'm done.

It's easy to forget it's raining when inside—unless I'm watching the dripping ceiling or the buckets fill up with water, which I can't remember starting. *Has it always been that way?* —but once I'm out on the porch, the dreary drip, drip, drip of the rain off the eaves is about to drive me mad. Is it ever going to stop?

Pacing, my eyes dart down to the dock, willing Nick and the boat to be there to take me back to reality, but of course, it's empty. Tears prick the corner of my eyes and I clench my fists. What the hell ever compelled me to want to be alone on some godforsaken island in the middle of nowhere? Screaming in frustration, I drag my fingers through my hair before roughly sliding them over my face. When my eyes open, there is movement on the perimeter of my vision, and seconds later, the woman, the ghost, is clearly in view.

Fed up with the cat-and-mouse game we have going on, I call out to her. "Hey!"

She doesn't even acknowledge me, her usual response to anything I say.

"Hey! I'm talking to you! Who are you?"

She stops walking, so I must have gotten her attention. I know that's the case when she turns her head slightly toward me.

"Yes, you! Listen, I'm sorry. I'm in a bad mood right now. This house . . ." I trail off as I think about what Ari said and about the craziness of the last week. Trying again, I call out, "Hey, is there a boat on the island?"

The woman hesitates for a moment before her legs once again start working and she heads to the water.

"I'm sick of this! Talk to me, damn it! What do you *want*? You obviously want me to see you, right? What do you want to say?" Again, she has stopped, and I know she's listening. I pause to give her some time to answer. And while I wait, I try to study her. She's corporeal, as far as I can tell. She's not flickering in and out of view, and she hasn't disappeared. She's solid . . . just like all the other times I've seen her. I move to the porch steps and watch. Even though it's mainly her back I see with just a partial view of her profile, I'm close enough to see the rise and fall of her shoulders as she takes a breath. But she refuses to say a word.

"Just get it over with and *tell* me already!" I yell. I know she wants me to see her. What I don't understand is why she won't just spill it already. *Maybe she can't?*

Instead of talking to me, she stands in front of the water looking out into the distance. Her long, curly hair lifts in the slight breeze and it's only now I realize the rain, pouring in sheets just moments ago, has stopped once again. I can hear the water as it laps up onto the shore and as it slaps at the seasoned wood of the empty dock. The sound only enhances the silence of the rest of the world.

"Please talk to me," I exhale as I start down the steps toward the woman. "Will you at least look at me?"

To my surprise, she does. Quickly, she glances at me, determining how far away I am from her. Her toe touches the water as if she's testing the temperature.

Encouraged by her glance, I try again. "Can you wait for a minute? Can you just stop?" Tears come unbidden, and I struggle to keep my voice even. "I'm tired, you know?" I double my pace as I see her raise her foot and plunge it into the water. "I-I just want to go home now. I'm done."

The woman nods slowly, her hair moving on her shoulders as her head bobs up and down. She takes a few more steps, her ankles now disappearing under the gently lapping waves. She turns toward me again; her face is a blur to me, so focused I am on the emotion in her tear-rimmed eyes.

"It's time. I'm so sorry," she whispers. She turns toward the water again, her steps more determined as she wades out.

Snapped out of the spell cast by her tears by her sudden forward movement, I too step forward, my sandal touching the water's edge. Hissing, I pull back. It's just water. I've done this before. I've done this. But I can't shake the feeling that if I go in, something bad will happen, something that makes me tremble with fear.

I glance up at the woman who is now chest-deep. Her hair which had been dancing on the wind now pulls down, weighted by the water touching the ends.

"What are you doing? Hey! Look, I don't swim, and you're making me kind of nervous, so could you come back, please?"

Frantically, I search for someone to aid me. "Hammond!" I scream. "Gail!" Here, this woman is going to commit suicide right in front of me and there is nothing I can do to stop her. *But she's a ghost.* I replay all the times she has disappeared, and even with that logic, I'm standing here watching as she wades deeper and deeper into the water. I can't just let it happen. "Help me!" I scream as I run back toward the house, only to turn back and run toward the water as it rises to the woman's neck. "Ari! Someone!"

I kick off my shoes. I can do this. I can save her, and before I can think anything of it, I push forward, feeling the cool water on my calves as I sprint toward her.

I look around, but the surface is clear now. She's gone under. Screaming for help again, I splash forward, the water up to my thighs. I'm crying now, hot, fat tears mixing with the drops of water that splash my face as I search the lake. Sobbing, I try to scream again, but terror grips me as I think of all the things that could be lurking underneath the surface. Creatures I can't see, hands that are ready to pull me under the depths. I can't move forward. I can't help her. She's going to die because of me.

Where were Hammond and Gail? "Help me, please!" I scream, and my hands tentatively start grabbing at the water before suddenly I'm hysterically moving it with my hands, my arms, too afraid to move forward with my feet, and bending to get every inch I possibly can.

A flash of pale-yellow fabric catches my anxious eyes, and my gaze latches onto that stretch of the lake. Simultaneously trying to pull it toward me with my arms while making a wiping gesture as if it would make the muddy water any clearer, I search for a glimpse of the fabric again.

"Please!" I shout to God and the universe and am rewarded with another glimpse just ahead of me, just out of reach. Without thinking, I step forward, snatching the fabric and pulling it into a tight fist. Gasping for breath, I make my way back to the shore, walking backward as my feet slip on the mossy bedrock of the lake bottom.

At one point, I careen back, nearly losing my balance. My hands come up out of the water and act as counterweights until I feel my feet firmly placed. Terrified I have lost the woman to the lake again, my hands lunge into its depths, immediately grasping anything within reach. Whimpering with relief, I feel the fabric and again head back to the shore, no more than three feet behind me.

She's dead weight. And even though she hasn't been in the water that long—*how long has it been anyway?*—her pale-yellow shirt clings to her torso now that we're out, and I can tell she's not breathing. Again, I scream for help. Do these people never look out the window?

Bending down, I turn the woman over onto her back and put my ear to her chest to listen for her heart. I think that's what you're supposed to do? My mind races through all the CPR videos I had to watch while training to be a lifeguard—*wait. Lifeguard?* I shake my head. I hate water, I was never a lifeguard. Tendrils of hair are plastered to the woman's face and as I brush them aside to do mouth-to-mouth, my eyes wander to her closed ones, and I take in her entire face in an instant. I never saw it clearly because she was always walking away from me, always headed—suddenly any breath I was about to give to the woman disappears and I'm wheezing as I spring away from her.

This can't be real. This isn't happening. My heart hammering in my chest, I inch forward to verify what my mind is telling me can't possibly be true. And then there is silence. Gone is the sound of the water lapping onto the shore, the tide coming in. Gone are the caws of the birds as they fly gracefully from tree to tree. All there is, is this moment. Me and her. Lyn. How can it be?

As I work over her, trying to breathe life back into her body, I think about the times I've seen her—this ghost—and how all the times I've seen her, Lyn hasn't once been with me. I check for a pulse and, finding none, I start chest compressions. "Don't do this to me, Lyn," I scream at her. "Don't you *dare* do this to me—Help! Please, someone, help me!" I scream, my throat raw from my shouts. I look about me frantically, but the lakefront remains empty. I pull Lyn to me, almost clawing at her to get her as close to me as possible. "I'm sorry, I'm sorry, I'm sorry, I'm sorry," I sob. "I'm so sorry."

I rock her back and forth, trying to comfort her, trying to comfort me. And laying her back on the ground, I start compressions again. That's when something clicks in my head, like a light switch has been turned on, or mental floodgates have been lifted, and all of a sudden, I'm swarmed with memories. *Compression*: I'm in the backyard playing when a guy comes along with a heavy-looking sack. I run screaming into the house to get my mom. *Compression*: I'm watching *The Wizard of Oz* with no fear until the flying monkeys appear. *Compression*: I'm walking through the woods in the rain, feeling like crap but knowing I'll feel better when I get home. Suddenly, I'm falling through the planks of an old bridge . . .

I stop compressions and wipe the hair from Lyn's face, not really paying attention because I'm too busy looking for someone to help me, too confused as well as to why I'm seeing her memories. "Help me!" I scream again, my voice muffled by sobs. Lyn's face is blurred by my tears, and hair covers her mouth. I push it aside gently before wiping my tears so I can start mouth-to-mouth.

I lean forward, inhaling sharply, and my heart feels as if it's trying to rip itself from my chest. *What'll I do if I lose my mirror?* "Don't leave me," I plead as I smooth her hair, so like mine, back away from her face and neck. "We're a package deal, remember? Where you go, I go?" I throw my head back and scream as loud as I can, praying someone will hear me. Forget about words; I'm all out of them, especially if she's taken from me. I pinch her nostrils and give two quick breaths in her mouth. Looking to her chest, I wait for it to fall as she exhales.

It doesn't come.

I pinch my nose . . . I mean her nose to start . . . *Wait, what?* When I lower my eyes, Lyn is more than a mirror. Lyn's not Lyn, she's me. I mean, I'm her.

Reaching out, I touch her—*my*—face. Abruptly, more memories fill my mind. Memories I haven't thought about in ages, people I haven't seen in what feels like a lifetime. I chuckle through my tears. I *was* a lifeguard, back in college during summer vacations. I almost lived in the water, I was around it so often. And after the bridge accident, when dancing on land had been taken away from me, I realized I could still dance in the water. So that's what I did. Synchronized swimming. It wasn't professional, but it allowed me to do what I loved when I wasn't helping people as a swim instructor. I touch her—my—cheek. I'm not looking at Lyn—a woman who I'm realizing never existed outside my mind. I'm looking at me . . . Me.

"I'm so sorry," I say, realizing I'm echoing what was said moments ago.

In the blink of an eye, it all makes sense. I remember everything, how it all happened, the accident that sent me here. I understand now. I'm reminded of Lyn's words back in the attic when she spoke to Hammond. *Did a part of me realize it back then?* I understand. *Maybe it's not too late.*

"I'm afraid it is."

I startle at the voice beside me. Nick has appeared out of nowhere, and I stupidly look to the dock expecting to see his boat, but the dock is still decidedly empty.

"What do you mean? I can revive her—me!"

"Why didn't you ever come out with me?

"What?" I ask, exasperated. "Nick, what are you talking about? I tried—"

"Yes, you tried, and I so wanted you to succeed."

"I was so afraid—" My voice cuts as I glance down at my soaked pale-yellow tunic and white Capri shorts. I know he's not talking about the lunches over the last few days, but about something else entirely. I just can't figure it out quite yet. "I-I—" My eyes jump from one thing to the next, landing on nothing to keep me focused. "Nick, this isn't helping!" I deflect. "Help me, will you?"

I shove up my sleeves and then push soaked tendrils of hair out of my face. I put my hands together, ready to do chest compressions, and look down.

There's no one on the beach besides Nick and me.

Desperately I turn this way and that before looking down once again, freezing when the reality of this highly surreal experience kicks in. They were both different facets of me—the ghost, Lyn. I glance down at my outfit again, the same outfit as the me I pulled out of the water—pale-yellow fabric. I realize now I've been wearing it every day since I've been here. Sitting down hard, I turn to Nick.

"But I can save me, right?"

"You had work to do." Nick sighs. "Relax, reflect, release," he nods. "Trying to save a life. That's what you're trying to do, what you've been trying to do, and you didn't even realize it. The mind works in mysterious ways, don't you think? What do they call it? Putting your affairs in order. It's truly extraordinary when you think about it."

"Wait, what? You're not making any sense, Nick. You're not." I shake my head vehemently as I look at him, but I can't help noticing only the truth staring back at me. "This is my mind!" I cry. "Right? So, I can just will myself to wake up."

Nick shakes his head sadly. "I wish it were that simple."

The dock draws my attention, and because I have to do something, I get up and walk over to it. The sun, that beautiful orb I'm only now realizing is only there when things must be physically calm, is low on the horizon and the waves continue their ceaseless attack on the wooden pilings. Walking onto it, I head toward its edge. "That was the way back, wasn't it?" I ask, my voice hollow.

I think back to the times Nick casually asked me to go out for lunch or to go for a boat ride. "Wasn't it?"

When Nick doesn't say anything, I know I've hit upon it. "I'll go with you now. Let's go," I say. I snap my fingers, trying to conjure the boat. "I'm not afraid."

"It's too late." Nick has followed me over, and he stands with his head tipped back as if he's trying to absorb the last of the sun's rays.

"What do you mean, it's too late? I'm in my head, so there must be a part of me that's still alive. I'm like, in a coma or something, right?"

Silence.

"Why the hell make me so afraid of the water if that was the only way back?"

Nick gives a soft snort. "It's ironic, isn't it?" he says. "You aren't afraid of living as you thought, but you were afraid of facing your own death. Only when you could come to terms with what happened to you, could you move forward."

I think of when I stepped on the dock and the images of the boat that were so clear. "So, I'm just going to give up?

Because of some freak accident while I was trying to help someone—He fell overboard!" I spin on Nick, my brows furrowed and my nostrils flared. "I should have just let him drown? My fucking job landed me here?" And then I snort. "This can't be it."

Silence.

"Then why did you come here to begin with? What was the point of all this?" I wave my hands around, indicating the scenery.

"That's an age-old question, isn't it? It goes along with 'why is there life? Why do anything at all?'" Nick stares at me, his eyes wide, willing me to respond with the answer he is looking for. All I can do is stare in return, my mind whirring.

"To survive!" Nick enunciates emphatically. "We fight like hell to live! I'm your desire for life. I'm here because you don't want to let go. Eve, you never gave up on life. Sometimes, shit just happens." His words echo what Lyn said, what *I* knew myself all along.

"I don't accept that," I snap.

Nick looks down at the water. Taking a penny out of his pocket, he flips it between his fingers for a few moments before tossing it into the lake. After a few minutes more, he nods and then turns to me with a sigh. "Sometimes the party is in full swing when it's time to go. You don't want to leave, but you still have to."

## Chapter 30

So Lyn never existed. I'm still having a hard time coming to terms with it. My name is Evelyn Beckett. Eve and Lyn, two sides of the same coin. Lyn may not have been my twin, but I do have a sister, Emma. We aren't twins in the actual sense, but my parents had the two of us close together, and we were always getting into all sorts of mischief when younger.

I wonder how she's handling this. She had wanted me to ditch the retirement party on the yacht and go with her to a supposedly haunted mansion. She's always been into that sort of thing. I look back at the house. I remember her showing me a newspaper article, and I'm sure that's where the idea of this house and the ghost came from.

We have our differences— are there siblings who don't? —but we're there for each other. Except, I hadn't thought about her once, not until today. Talk about self-absorbed.

I want to be there for her. Hold her. Tell her I love her. The "Lyn" part of me reminded me how frustrating and how close Emma and I can be. I know she has her own life to live, that she'll get through this just fine. If I do die, she'll probably start doing seances to try to talk to me. I chuckle because that is so Emma, but I hope it won't be the case. I'm hoping I can still get through this, and if I can't, well, she deserves more than a life chasing an echo. I sigh and thank God she's not the one here.

Then there are my parents. I'm glad they have each other and my sister. After my bridge accident, my mom didn't leave my side for about a week. My heart hurts for what this will do to her.

But I'm still half-convinced I'll wake up at some point. I mean, I'm still here, and Nick is still around, so even though he's all gloom and doom now, it has to account for something. I also wonder about Ari. What is his role in all of this? Is he just another figment of my imagination, another facet of myself like the ghost and Lyn? In some ways, I wish Lyn was still here. I would talk to her about this, and she would give me some rational advice or something.

I snigger. The whole time I've been here, I've thought about wanting to get away from myself but relishing the comfort I gained whenever I talked to myself. Is that a definition of insanity? Well, no one can say I'm not comfortable in my own head.

My feet, ankles, and calves dangle in the water as I sit on the edge of the dock. I'm no longer afraid, and the water feels wonderful. I feel a presence beside me, and when I turn, Lyn is sitting there.

"I didn't think I'd see you again, seeing as"—I air quote—"'You are me and I am you.'"

Lyn smiles. "Ahhh, you got it. I was wondering if you would figure it out." She pauses, the smile slipping from her face. "Apparently, you still have some things you need to think through. If seeing another 'person'"—she mirrors my air quotes from moments ago— "helps make it easier for you, I am here."

"So, I'm doing this." I wave my hand over her form.

"Of course, you are." She gives me a *duh* look before swishing her legs in the water.

"I don't want to die." I don't hear any fear in my voice. I'm just stating a fact. I don't know if I'm beyond fear at this point or if I'm still in shock. After all, I did just figure out I'm dying.

Lyn sighs and then shrugs like dying is no big deal. "You could still fight it, you know. I mean, you must be fighting it, right, or else you wouldn't be here?"

"You've got a point there." I perk up, extra determined to figure out a way out of my head and get back to living my life. I know now there are so many things I'll do differently. And the first thing of all will be to hug my mom extra tight.

"I—and by extension, you—can be pretty smart when I want to."

I grin over at her. "I believe you." I take in her appearance, wondering how my brain had tricked me into thinking I had a twin in the first place. Our outfits have changed. It's like once I understood all the subtle hints my brain was trying to tell me to force my realization of my condition, I stopped needing to see them. Gone, the pale-yellow fabric. Instead, I'm wearing red, my favorite color. Lyn's wearing black. "But you don't sound very enthusiastic."

Lyn bites her lip. "I'm tired. Dying, or I guess I should say trying to live, takes a lot out of you."

I snort. "Even on a regular day when you're not fighting for every breath."

Lyn laughs too.

"I'm not in any pain."

"You have Gail and Hammond to thank for that."

"They're me too, aren't they?

"A part of you, yes. They're doing what they can to keep you comfortable."

The house stands tall, silent, and a bit worse for wear when I turn toward it. Ari had said the owner might be locking its doors. I guess the house is me too. All the images of moisture, the buckets of water Gail was always carrying, the mold and mildew, the sopping wet furniture, make complete sense now. All of them hints to help me figure out what was going on. "Relax, reflect, release," I say.

"I guess we've moved on to the *reflect* portion of our retreat."

"What am I supposed to reflect on now? I've already thought of my family. If I keep thinking of them, all I'm going to do is have regrets, think about things I should have said, things I should have done. I don't want to live my final moments that way."

"If they are your final moments."

"You really think there's still a chance?"

"Don't you?"

"I don't know what to think anymore. All of a sudden, everything is about me, and I'm not used to it."

"Yeah, you do tend to think about others a lot, thinking about what you're doing to them. The way you kept apologizing to me. Apologizing to yourself. Why did you do that?"

"Because I've let myself down," I say, forcing myself to look into my own eyes.

"How so?"

"Ever since the bridge accident, I've been living too carefully. You said it yourself; I wasn't living, I was hiding. I was too busy being responsible that I didn't take enough chances in life. And now it might be too late."

"So, what do you want to say?"

"I want to say I'm sorry!"

"No," Lyn shakes her head firmly. "You've said that enough. Maybe it's something you want to hear?"

"I want to hear that you forgive me." I think about the retirement party. "I knew it was a risk when I jumped in after him . . . So many people were telling me not to do it. There were rocks under the water we couldn't see, but he was young." I pause to collect my thoughts and swish my legs through the water once more. "And I kept thinking about redemption, thinking that saving him would save me, help me overcome my fears." I glance at Lyn. "Does that make sense?" I look back out toward the water and don't wait for a response. "I want to know that it wasn't all a waste. I want to know that if I come back from this, I'll move forward with a new lease on life."

"And if you don't?"

"Well, then I want to know it wasn't all in vain. I did my best. I did what I knew would keep me safe in order to live, to survive. It may not have been enough, but it was my best."

"I forgive you."

I smile at her sadly. "I finally forgive me too."

➤ The House on the Lake

## Chapter 31

Sitting on the wide porch steps, I stare out at the water, thinking of everything and nothing at the same time. Now that I know what's going on, things are different. The sun is no longer low on the horizon, nor is it dark. Instead, the sky is a bright blue, the sun high in the sky, its rays sparkling off the waves in tiny points of light.

Nick sits next to me, mute, his fingers playing with the bottom of his tie. He rolls it up, then unrolls it only to repeat the procedure. He doesn't say anything. He doesn't have to. I'm basically waiting for the inevitable. I know it's coming. I've always known it. I just thought I'd have more time.

Resigned, I stand up, sighing loudly. I squint at the lake and understand now why I've never seen anyone on it besides Nick.

"Where are you going?"

"It's time to face the music," I say as I move toward the open front door. I have to talk to Ari. I turn back to Nick, but he's already gone.

\*\*\*

Because I'm not exactly sure what I'm going to say to him when I see him, and because I don't know where he is anyway, I decide to take a peek around the house once more. Even though I know what's happening, it still takes me by surprise when I start to look—really look—at the house around me.

I settle on going up to the attic first when I stop on the landing of the grand staircase. A water stain, bigger than ever, is taking over half of the landing. Not only that, but the walnut surfaces appear dull and lifeless, an almost grayish silver tinge cast over any part that had been exposed to the sun through the glass windows at the staircase landing. Those parts that haven't been exposed are drab and unpolished.

Where before the stained-glass and iron window, though somewhat dusty, could clearly be seen as a work of art, now it's hard to define where one piece ends and the next begins, so heavy with grime the smaller pieces have become, and several of the larger pieces of glass are missing from the panels.

When I reach the attic, I'm relieved to see it isn't deteriorating. Everything appears to be intact, the same as it did that first day I came up here with Lyn. The unusual painting above the fireplace and all the portraits and landscapes still hang on the walls. I take a deep breath and begin walking around the room when a picture to the left of the chimney catches my attention. My eyes furrow. It wasn't like that before.

The picture in question is much more recent than any I had seen—or thought I had seen—in here before, and when I reach it, I can't help but take a step back, my hand covering my mouth when I gasp. Gail's words come back to me as I step forward to look at the picture again: *Sometimes people don't make the best decisions in life.*

It's a photo from maybe nine years ago. I had caught my boyfriend at the time cheating on me. Instead of walking away from what would end up being another three months of lies and betrayal, I had forgiven him. Looking back, I can totally see it for the bad decision it was, but at the time I thought I loved him.

I had called a friend over to cheer me up and told her I needed a change. She tried to convince me to leave him. I was too busy convincing myself she was wrong. Instead of changing the guy, I had changed the wallpaper—the exact same wallpaper in the kitchen downstairs. *What kind of day was she having when she picked* this *out?*

I look at another picture, a photograph of my mother. Another one shows me in the bathtub when I was two or three. Bubbles fill the tub, and only my head and a hand holding on to a yellow rubber duck can be seen above the white suds.

Moving to another wall, I see myself at different ages, under different circumstances. In more than one, I'm crying or I'm angry. In several, I'm smiling or laughing. I know these pictures were never taken because I remember all these moments. This one is of Beth, my best friend from childhood, and me riding our bikes down Thorndyke, the street on which we both lived. And this one is when I'm no more than five. My Grandma is sticking out her false teeth and making me laugh hysterically. All of them are memories, and I can't help but smile even as tears sting the back of my eyes.

I'm still taking them all in when I hear a soft cough behind me.

"There you are," I say. Ari stands just inside the doorway, his hands clasped behind his back. I guess I thought I would be mad at him, but there is no anger.

"Here I am," he says, and that stupid little crinkle at the corner of his eyes deepens. My heart still beats a little faster upon seeing him, and my stomach still feels as it does right at the top of a rollercoaster when the cars start to fall or in an elevator right as it begins its descent.

"You aren't real, are you?" I don't even know why I'm asking. I already know.

"I am exactly who and what you need me to be," he says as he takes a couple of steps and leans against the wall.

I scrub my face, look around at all the pictures of me, and snort. "Great, I'm a complete narcissist."

Ari guffaws and then comes over to me and rubs my arms before pulling me into a hug. "Well, we all have to love ourselves, right?" he asks as he pulls back to gaze into my eyes.

"Yeah, well, this is taking things to a whole other level, don't you think?"

Ari laughs again.

"When did you know?"

"Well, before you did, your conscious self at least."

"This is so weird."

"Don't think of it that way. I'm not just a figment of your imagination. It's a little more complicated than that. I mean, you were obviously trying to figure things out, and I helped you do that, but I'm not just in your head."

"What do you mean?"

Ari rubs his forehead, then rakes his hands through his hair. "Have you talked to Nick?"

"Yeah, we've talked," I say, wondering where this is going.

"You never went with him."

"I tried! I was so afraid of the water—and then, it seemed like every time I was determined to try, the weather would freak out—"

"I'm not blaming you! I'm asking you to think about it a bit more." Ari holds on to one of my hands and pulls me over to the rocking chair, pushing me gently into it before he sits in front of it on the floor.

I sink back into the cushion covering the back before responding. "He basically told me he represents my desire to live."

"Were you ever attracted to him?" Ari could be talking about what he had for dinner last night with the amount of jealousy I *don't* hear. For him, it's just a question, and although it digs at my gut that he can be so nonchalant, I blush anyway.

"Well, yeah. He's a good-looking guy." I smile. "He's smart, funny . . . he's attractive . . . Wait, are you saying he's attractive because life is attractive to me?" I angle myself so I'm able to observe Ari's face. "What does that say about you then?" I touch his cheek. "But there was something different about you. It was like I was drawn to you."

His blue eyes are intense as he looks at me. "What did you think of me when you first saw me?"

I blush again, a deeper shade of crimson. "I already told you . . . It doesn't matter, it—"

Ari's hand comes up to softly grip my knee and I look down at it before lifting my head, so I have to look him in the eye. "Tell me. I want to know," he interrupts, his voice low and husky, his gaze straying to my lips and his fingers caressing my leg.

"You're . . . you're magnificent," I whisper, leaning forward. And right then, as so often I feel when I'm around him, I'm a starstruck idiot, my eyes adoring, my words sappy. I can't help it. I lean away and try to compose myself. "There was this air of mystery around you," I say. "I told you I was afraid. This voice in the back of my head kept telling me to be careful." I stare at a table in front of us, the plastic, dust-covered leaves of a plant nearly touching the wooden surface. "I mean . . ." and then it all clicks, and I don't understand why it didn't earlier. "Ari, how old are you?"

His head jerks up and I can tell he knows where my thoughts are headed. "That's the thing, I've been here since the beginning," he says with a sigh.

"And what does that mean, exactly?" I ask. "The beginning of what?"

Ari rakes his hand through his hair. "I don't know how to explain it. I don't even know if I understand it all. I just know that I've always been here. I'll always be here. What is time? I know the concept. I know minutes, hours, years, but at the same time—no pun intended—it means very little to me."

And now it's my turn to be fascinated. I can do nothing but stare. I have no idea how to process this information. "So, are you alive or dead?"

Ari nods his head before shaking it. "Both?" he suggests questioningly before his eyes light up. "Have you ever heard of Schrodinger's cat?"

Memories of a mandatory physics class come to mind. "I think so, but remind me."

Ari narrows his eyes as he gathers his thoughts. "Schrodinger says that if you put a cat in a box with something that could kill the cat, like a radioactive atom that could decay or not based on the amount of time it's in the box, and you sealed the box up, you wouldn't know if the cat was alive or dead until you opened the box."

"Nice guy, that Schrodinger," I say. "I hope he didn't have any animals."

"What I'm *trying* to say," Ari smirks, "is I'm kind of in that box. I could be alive or dead, but I've been in this box the whole time, so I don't know."

"It would depend upon the observer then. And since I'm observing you, you're alive." I almost want to pat myself on the back, but the answers I know are forthcoming have my heart rate elevated and my muscles tense.

"That's certainly possible, but you're here at Lakeview Manor, so it's quite possible you're in the box too." He smiles. "And here we're talking about boxes again."

I smile too, but don't lose my focus. "So, you don't remember a time when you weren't here?"

Ari tilts his head back and forth. "It's a bit more complicated than that, but the short answer is no."

"How is that possible? Lakeview Manor isn't that old."

"It's not just about Lakeview. There are lots of . . . houses."

"And time doesn't mean anything to you?"

"Not really, but as far as this conversation goes, it's neither here nor there."

Ari gets up and walks across the room to look at the pictures, but I know he's just giving me time to process everything, to come to the conclusion my brain keeps skimming over but refuses to land on. I think back to when I met Ari, how he told me the house may need to be closed. I think about his argument with Nick, and about who Nick is. Then I think about my scare in the attic, how the ghost I thought I was looking at turned out to be me, and how the actual ghost of the woman turned out to be me as well. Lakehouse is me. I already knew it, but this just makes the reality that much clearer. I already know I'm dying, so Ari is . . .

"You're Death?"

Ari turns toward me slowly, his eyes hooded. He bites the inner corner of his mouth before answering. "Close enough, I guess."

I feel void of any emotion, just numb, and I fleetingly wonder if this is what actual death will feel like before I remember how the man in front of me has made me feel anything but dead. "Why didn't you tell me?"

Ari shakes his head, snorting and sneering at the same time. "Yeah, that would have gone over well," he says, laughing snidely. "Hello, I'm Death, or pretty much its representative. Let's hang out, get to know one another."

I narrow my gaze, and a chill comes over me. "So, you decide to misrepresent who you are instead."

Ari's eyes widen. "When did I ever do that?" He moves closer, his arms outstretched, but it's my turn to turn away. I don't want to hear what he has to say. I don't want any of this.

Ari's voice is softer when he continues. "Eve, it's one thing I would never do. There's no point. You were bound to meet me one day or another. I don't decide when. I'm just here when it happens. Some people meet me more than once. They're able to come back, either by medical intervention or the grace of something bigger than us all."

I think about the secret room Ari led me to, how he told me the other door would one day unlock just for me. "You had me find the door," I say as I search his face for any indication of deception.

"It's your house. Only you knew where the room was."

"But you knew," I say, my brows furrowing. I think back to our conversation, how as I sat on the bed, he stood next to the closet door, eventually moving to sit in front of it, tapping his head against it as if silently communicating where it was.

"I had no idea. It's different for everyone, after all." Sensing my confusion, Ari offers more. "It's possible your subconscious wanted you to figure it out. That's essentially what the room is."

As interesting as I'm sure the psychology behind it all is, I've already jumped ahead, my next question coming out in a rush. "So, I can beat this?"

Ari's eyes become sad. "Yes, and as much as I hate to say it, for selfish reasons, this could be one of those times where we just pass in the night. There's that possibility, but Eve—"

I hate the hurt and sadness I see in his eyes, but he's a part of me, who I need him to be—at least a part of him is. He's already said as much, so I can't allow myself to think about what he's feeling—or what I'm feeling? —or what it could suggest about my psyche.

"Nick doesn't think it's possible. But there has to be a chance, even if it's a small one. Don't take this away from me, Ari. I like you, probably more than I should, but I don't want to die. I'm not ready."

"I know you're not," says Ari. "But is anyone ever ready? I'm not here to push you, Eve, and the last thing I want is for you to think I am, but I also want you to know that sometimes you don't have a choice . . . and if this happens to be that time, please know it's because it's your time. It has nothing to do with me. I have no say."

"Then why the hell did you get me to like you so much? Are you saying I have some sort of death wish or something?

I want to die? I don't! I'm supposed to have a relationship—with an actual person!" I say, staring at him hard. "I'm supposed to fall in love, maybe a couple of times, and, and I don't know, *do* something with my life!"

Ari sighs. "I don't know, Eve. I don't know. Maybe . . . maybe your liking me gives you the chance to have a relationship? I don't want that to be—that is, I hope that's not the case because it would be really nice for you to like me for me."

Silence envelops the room as I think about his words. Who's saying them really? Is there this personification of death in my head who feels something for me, or is it my brain trying to get me to reconcile and accept the fact that I'm dying? Ari's eyes are filled with anguish. How many times has he had to give this speech to hopeful people who just want to see their loved ones again, have another birthday, have just one more day?

"Do I have a say?"

"When it's time, it's time, but how do you know if you don't give it a shot and try?"

"Ari . . ." I hesitate. Different aspects of our conversation echo through my mind, but the look in his eyes and the fact that I want to launch myself into his arms have one facet hovering in the forefront. "What's between us—is it . . . real?"

Ari stands before me and caresses my cheek, his eyes earnest. "Eve, I may be in your head, but I don't know what you're thinking. I don't know how you feel about me. And I won't lie; my relationship with every individual is an intimate one. It kind of has to be with what I do." He shrugs. "But I have never, ever felt like this with anyone." He kisses me firmly and pulls me into his arms. "That, I swear to you."

# Chapter 32

**I** don't know what to say. A part of me must have known this because, well, because Ari is me and I am Ari—only, a part of Ari is Death, which isn't a part of me but a part of so much more. Ugh, so confusing!

I step away and look into Ari's eyes. I'm not shocked. I get it. Somehow, my brain has processed it all, and even though I can't coherently think about it logically, it's all there, all understood.

But I'm angry. I didn't ask for this. I didn't want this. And what does it mean if I'm drawn to Death, if that's who Ari, in some roundabout way, is? I should just accept it? Maybe I would if I was old or sick, but I wasn't. I'm *not*. I'm a twenty-eight-year-old woman who would like to be in a real relationship someday, maybe have a kid or two. I just paid off my car, and I'm supposed to be in my best friend's wedding next month.

I pace. "You and Nick are brothers, so death is a part of life. I get that. And you've shown me I don't have to fear it, and I appreciate that more than you know, but I don't want this right now."

Ari inhales sharply as if I've punched him, and suddenly he's angry. "Glad to know you *appreciate* me. That just makes all of this so swell." He clasps his hands together dramatically as though he's in one of those sappy movies where everything ends perfectly, and then he glares at me.

Flabbergasted, I turn around in a circle and then look at him pointedly. "I don't know what to think right now! You tear families apart, take life when—"

"No!" The word is harsh, guttural. "No. I don't do that. *People* do that, accidentally or otherwise. Disease does that, malnutrition, hunger. Not me. I'm just a guide, Eve." Ari rakes his fingers through his hair and gives an exasperated sigh. "I only show people the way after all is said and done. I don't *take* anything. I don't revel in a person's passing."

I stalk over to one of the floor-to-ceiling windows with a view of the lake, taking deep breaths to calm myself. The lake is as calm as it always is, despite the storm clouds closing in from the west.

"I'm not forcing you to do anything. You know that, right? At no moment will I push you to do anything. I won't coax you or try to lure you, but *when* the time comes—and it comes for everyone—I'll be there to hold your hand. You won't be alone."

His words are a comfort to me; the knowledge that something so huge as the end of all I know will be faced with someone by my side has me breathing easier. But it doesn't erase the fact that I'm not ready. There has to be something I can do.

"I want to live," I whisper, and the tears pricking the back of my eyes help me realize just how true this statement is. "I want to live," I say louder, turning around to face Ari. "I'm sorry. I'm so sorry. You mean more to me than mere appreciation. You have to believe that. Getting to know you . . . you've helped me learn a lot about myself, and I can't imagine . . ." How can I convey everything I want to say? I can't. Not at this moment. Not when there's so much I still have left to do. "This can't be how it ends for me."

Ari is silent, and after a moment, he nods his head slowly. Coming over to me, he rests his hands on my shoulders and waits until my eyes raise to his. "I would never try to stop you," he says. "I'll be here when you're ready . . . whenever that is."

As if there is a balloon within me that deflates, all my remaining frustration dissipates, and I'm left feeling a sense of gratitude. I don't know if I'll ever be ready to stop wanting what I have, to stop fighting for it, but knowing he'll be here when it's time is reassuring.

"Hardly anyone wants to meet me," Ari says with a small smile, "but I'm not a bad guy."

"No, you're not," I agree. "Does everyone shy away from you? That must be incredibly lonely."

"Not everyone. Some people feel accomplished in all they've done. They have no regrets, so they walk with me willingly." Ari's smile widens. "I wish that for you, Eve. One day you'll take my hand and walk with me and know, deep down, that you did everything you could and lived life the best way you knew how. That's the best way."

I lean into him, my forehead on his chest. I don't want to be upset anymore. I was never one to believe that Death handpicked those who died. And if getting to know Ari more is how it's going to end someday, I can live with it . . . no pun intended.

"So, how long have you been doing this, again?" I ask as I swipe at a tear.

Ari smirks. "Nice try."

I smile. "Well, have you ever 'worked' with someone famous? How old was the oldest person? Do you have a sickle? No, don't tell me. Do you know the Big Guy? Are there others? There must be others who work with you."

Ari continues to smile as I ply him with questions, and occasionally he laughs, but he doesn't give anything away. "I'll make you a promise," he says softly. "I'll tell you some day. Okay?"

This time I grin. "Well, I guess it's a promise I know I can hold you to."

And instead of feeling anxious that this could be the end for me, I'm instead filled with a sense of calmness.

I reach up to hug Ari tightly, accepting him for who I know him to be, feeling his warm body next to mine, and I know what home feels like. Abruptly, I break free from his arms and look up into his eyes again. There is sadness there and understanding, and love, and it hurts more than I thought it would to leave him standing here like this. I reach out to touch him once again when I freeze.

Something is different. A stillness that wasn't there before. The underlying sound I've grown so accustomed to is missing. It's—

"Something's wrong," I cry as I rush to the window once again. The storm clouds that were in the distance moments ago are right on top of the house, and the water in the lake is choppy and rough. My eyes race to Ari once again.

Ari's face is etched with concern, and he comes over to join me. His eyes grow distant for a moment before going wide. "Eve, you're running out of time. You—"

"I have to go!"

"Go!" he urges, but I'm already running from the room and tearing down the stairs that creak and moan as I race past. When I reach the ground floor, I head for the living room. The fastest route is to go through there and to the foyer beyond.

I pull on the front door and fall back when it doesn't budge. Surprised, I grunt as I land on the floor. What the hell? The door has always opened before. Getting up, I try again, pulling at the handle with increased vigor. When it still won't open, I run through the house until I reach the library and try the side door there.

I almost whimper in relief when it practically comes off its hinges with the strength I use to open it. And not even bothering to make sure it closes behind me, I run around the house toward the lake.

I feel like I'm running through fine sand as I pound toward the water, and each foot I gain seemingly takes twenty. The rain pouring from the sky only hinders my progress as puddles become obstacle courses, each one I must dodge or jump over, fearing its depth.

I can't let myself stop for breath, but my lungs ache and my legs burn, my body begging me to rest for a moment. I look up, checking the distance I still have to go, calculating how hard I'll have to swim just to get through the surf. My heart owns a doubt and I double my efforts.

Finally, I make it to the water's edge. It churns, spitting and swallowing itself in front of me, its dark depths hiding who knows what secrets and truths. I barely pause to kick off my sandals and forge ahead, the water licking my calves, my thighs, my torso, until I'm submerged to my neck.

Taking a deep breath, I dip beneath the waves, expecting the lake to be calmer. It's not. Algae tangles between my legs as it dances, swaying and jumping chaotically in syncopation with the storm above.

Attempting a front crawl, I push my arms before me, but the strength of the water keeps pulling my legs downward. Again and again, I force my body to move horizontally, pumping my legs as my arms pierce the water ahead and push it behind me. I continue until I feel my lungs about to burst and only then do I lift myself toward the sky, inhaling deeply when I reach the surface, my mouth filling with equal parts rain, the lake, and oxygen. Coughing roughly, I spit water out of my mouth and try to pull more air into my lungs.

I can feel fatigue in my limbs, and it would feel so nice to stop and rest for a moment, just half a second, but I know I have to continue. If I can make it away from the island, I'll wake up. I have to believe that.

Because I've been swimming for what seems like ages, I decide to look behind me, see how far away from the shore I am. I have to believe the distance I've come will give me the motivation I need to go on. *I'll look back in ten more strokes*, I tell myself. *Now only five.*

At two strokes to go, the muscles in my arms spasm, and I can hardly lift them out of the water, let alone pull water away from my body in an attempt to move forward. Stopping, I tread water, my breath ragged as I fight to inhale. I close my eyes and turn, anticipating the shore to be a hundred yards away but hoping I've paddled more than that.

Inhaling, I fight the urge to exhale, holding my breath to take a look. I squint, wiping water away from my eyes, and gasp. I lower my legs and sob when my toes just touch the bottom of the lake. Before me, the island sits, idyllically still in the raging tempest surrounding it, and the house looms above, so close I can almost feel its shadow fall upon me.

I turn away, my tears mixing with the rain and lake water, and plunge into the torrent once again. It can't end this way. It can't.

I move to a breaststroke. It's not as efficient but being as tired and out of breath as I am, I need to conserve my strength while still going the distance. That and I want to be able to see myself moving away from the island this time.

That was the hope. The reality is far different. The waves are so high, I'm lucky I can take in oxygen unless I push myself up above them, expending energy I don't have. Then when I *am* high enough to turn quickly and see, the rain is pelting down in sheets, preventing me from seeing anything of the island.

Drained, I tread momentarily before I push myself forward, ready to resort to the doggy paddle if I must. I can't go on anymore, not like this, and my body is so tired, I dare not even try to think of anything besides keeping my head above water. Something's gotta give!

Inevitably though, my legs sink, and my arms stop being useful, tossing water every which way as they flop on the water's surface like fish on dry land. Once again, my feet connect with the lake's rocky bottom, and as I turn back to the island, still just a stone's throw away, the only thing keeping me upright is the buoyancy of the surrounding water. Defeated, I allow the water to push me to shore, crawling when it's no longer high enough to hold me up.

I stop crawling when I can see individual granules of dirt swirling in inch-thick mud beneath me, and closing my eyes, I plop down on my back, turning my face to the side as I continue to breathe heavily.

"You gave it your best shot, you know."

Wheezing with the effort it's taking me to breathe in, and with my hand on my chest as if it will help to keep my lungs in place while they fill up with air, all I can do is open my eyes and glare at Nick as he sits next to me staring at the lake.

"Where . . . the hell . . . were you?" I pant. "I want . . . to live."

Nick turns from the lake and looks at me as if he's assessing my capabilities. "You can try again," he says nonchalantly, as if it hadn't taken every ounce of strength to give it a go the first—and second—time around.

I've never wanted to punch someone so badly in the face. "Can I have a minute?"

My sarcasm doesn't even phase him. He turns to face the lake again, and it's only then I notice it has stopped raining. The sky's still filled with dark, angry clouds, but it's as if they're waiting to see what I'll do.

"You're entitled to rest," he says softly, and this time when he looks at me, his eyes are filled with compassion. "No one's going to say you didn't fight."

"I'm not giving up," I sob. "I can do this." Pulling myself up onto all fours, I crawl back into the water. And the moment I do, the rain starts up again, beating down twice as hard as before, each drop a tiny dagger trying to penetrate my skin. "Come on!" I scream. I'm pissed. Suddenly, I'm plowing back into the water like I'm Poseidon himself, and this lake is nothing more than one of the puddles I dodged earlier.

As the rain pelts down, I glide through the water, rage filling my legs with the stamina to pump up and down relentlessly. *I think I can,* I puff as I remember the little engine my mom used to read to me about when I was young. *I know I can!* I continue to swim, my eyes closed, my movements methodical, my breath labored but stable. I don't know how long I've been at it now, minutes or hours. *This is nothing,* I say to myself. *It's a breeze!* Slowly, a smile spreads on my face. The water seems calmer. It doesn't feel as if I'm putting forth nearly as much effort as before. And on top of all that, it has stopped raining. My smile widens. I'm going to make it.

"If nothing else, it's nice to see you're not afraid of the water anymore."

I falter, miss a stroke. Nick's swimming with me?

"You going to say something?"

I jerk my eyes open only to stare in utter disbelief. Wooden columns jut out of the water next to me—the dock. Nick looks down at me from where he's seated on top of it, his feet dangling in the water. "No!" I howl. "No, no, no, no, no!" and as I'm screaming, Nick's pulling me up onto the dock. I open my eyes and Nick is next to me; his arms cradle me protectively.

"I can't do this anymore," I bawl. "I can't."

"I know."

"And it's so not fair. It's totally unfair," I snivel as I swipe at my tears.

"I know."

"And I love you," I say as I put my hands on his shoulders, my eyes staring into his. "You know that, right?"

Nick looks at me and smiles a smile so bright and warm, I nearly melt. "I know, and everyone knows it too."

"Why do I feel like I'm giving up?"

"You're not giving up, love," he says as he pulls me into his arms. "You just can't swim anymore."

## Chapter 33

My head doesn't feel as heavy as I make my way back toward land. I sit on the dock with Nick for a long time, watching as the storm clouds move off into the distance and watching the sun come out of hiding once again. We sit out there long enough for the dock to dry in most parts and for the water to quiet.

No words are necessary. It's just nice to *be*, and I think about the irony, now, so close to the end.

I don't want to turn from him. I don't want to be the one to walk away. But in this instance, he says I have to.

"I'm going to be here until the end," he says. I grasp his hand, squeezing tightly, fully intending to hold him to his promise.

Now that I've come to terms with everything, I'm kind of excited to start a new adventure, the way I felt when I went off to college or when I found out about my first—quote-unquote—real job.

"Do you know what will happen? After, I mean."

Nick follows me as we walk up to the manor. He shrugs. "What's the fun in knowing?" When he sees my disappointment, he expands a little. "It's different for everyone. Just like life." He nudges my shoulder. "You might even get to see me again. Whatever it is, Eve, it'll be great."

Lakeview. As I walk up the front steps to enter the house, Nick following close behind, I once again marvel at the change that has come over the place. One of the heavy wooden doors has come loose from its hinges; it leans precariously against the frame as if waiting to be reinstalled. The other creaks ominously as I open it.

The silence is overly loud. I feel a pull toward the secret room, and my feet lead me unerringly, even as my eyes try to take in everything within my surroundings, trying to hold on to each memory, every living thought.

Ari's in the room when we get there, just as I knew he would be. He's wearing a hooded cloak and stands just inside the door, radiating strength and power. His dark eyes lock onto my hand holding tightly to Nick's, but although I see his jaw clench, I also see compassion.

I squeeze Nick's hand while my eyes stay glued on Ari. "Can I talk to him alone for a moment?" I ask Nick. "You won't leave me?"

Nick squeezes back before letting go. "I'll be right here."

Taking a deep breath, I walk toward Ari and give him a smile.

"You had to wear the black cloak? Don't you think it's a bit cliché?"

"One time I wore it. One time, and it somehow became my signature piece. I wore it today because you expected me to." Ari lifts his hands, palms up, and I place mine within them. "Now who's being cliché?"

I rub my nose against his before stepping back to take in the surrounding room. It's unchanged, yet completely different. It's as if I'm looking at something I've always seen and always knew was there, but something has changed to make me see it differently. Maybe it's similar to how a parent is viewed as a child versus how that parent is seen as an adult. There is a shift, just as there's a shift now. I'm looking at everything with sharpened awareness. The rest of the house has disappeared, or might as well have for all that it matters to me now. All there is, is the room, Ari, and Nick.

"Are you ready?" Ari asks, his eyes filled with kindness and love.

"It's weird. I'm ready, but it's like . . . I had a really good friend in high school. We did everything together; there wasn't a day that went by where I didn't talk to her. Then, I left for college, and I knew when I hugged her goodbye that things would change. The love would still be there, but it would be different. I guess it's like that."

I think about my parents, who I know won't understand. After all, a parent should never have to lose a child, and I think about Lyn, my mirror. I know she was a part of me, a part that was always there but I didn't let many others see—not in a long while, at least—and now that I remember Emma, my real sister, it's not hard to understand why I got on so well with Lyn. Emma is a lot like her, like the me I used to be. Because of our closeness, I can't help but hope our bond somehow allows her to know, in this moment, how much she means to me. I wipe a tear away and take a deep breath. "I know everything and everyone will still be here, but my relationship with them will be different."

Ari bends to kiss my forehead. "I'm sorry it has to be this way."

"But that's life," Nick interrupts, joining us with a miserable smile.

As Ari holds me, I grasp one of Nick's hands. "I'm glad you're here with me, both of you."

"I won't leave," says Ari, and his arm moves from my shoulder so he can grab my other hand with his. We stand there, the three of us, and even the room fades away until all I see with complete certainty is the door that has remained locked.

"Did you know this whole time?" I don't know who I'm asking or what exactly. At this point, it doesn't really matter, but I'm curious just the same.

"We've been with you the whole time," says Nick. "Since the day you were conceived."

Ari nods. "There is always the possibility, so I too, have been here since the beginning. Waiting to meet you."

I laugh easily, understanding what he meant despite the way it sounded. "That's kind of creepy."

The corner of Ari's mouth lifts. "Yeah, I knew it when it came out of my mouth."

Nick snickers, and I relax even more.

In front of us, the door clicks. It's unlocked.

I take another deep breath. Fear and excitement building inside of me. This is the top of the rollercoaster right before the descent.

A strained giggle escapes. I'm afraid.

I squeeze Ari's hand more tightly and look up at him. We're entering his domain. His face is composed, happy even. *This* is life to him, home. There is no fear in his eyes, no hurt, no sadness. I take stock of my own feelings, what I can of the physical and emotional. There is no pain, not even worry. There is an awareness of what is to come and acceptance, pride in the life I have lived, and a willingness, albeit slightly reluctant, to let go.

"There's nothing to be afraid of. I'm here," he says.

"I know," I whisper.

A noise behind me has me turning to find Gail and Hammond, their eyes filled with sorrow. "We're sorry. We tried. We tried to help you."

I smile brightly. "I know you did. You've been helping me all along. Thank you."

Gail beams and Hammond gives a signature nod as they stand to the side, their fate irrevocably tied to mine.

Turning back to the door, I take a shaky breath. I'm holding on to both of them, each hand clenched to one of theirs. I don't want to let go of Nick, but I can't let go of Ari.

My head swivels to Nick and I squeeze his hand. I see everything and everyone I love in his eyes, and the beauty blinds me. But the beauty I see in Ari's eyes is just as blinding. The brilliance of the unknown just as glorious. A jolt passes through me, and I tighten my hold on both of them. There is life ahead of me and life behind me, and the life behind is the one I clutch onto with every fiber of my being because it's all

I've ever known. But there's curiosity about the one ahead, the one no one has come back to describe.

Even as I stand here, I fight the urge to walk through that door. When do I know it's time to accept the inevitable? At the very last?

Another jolt passes through me, and again my hands tighten to my lifelines. But I'm not afraid anymore. I don't ever have to be afraid again. I take a deep breath and give a final nod to both Ari and Nick. And then my hand loosens from one of theirs, and I feel his grasp slip, the sensation of his fingers on mine even after they've fallen away.

I have no regrets.

**The End**

➤ The House on the Lake

# Acknowledgements

There were times I didn't think I would make it to the acknowledgment page. From conception to completion, this book has reminded me of my kids, giving me gray hair and keeping me up at night. I worried about what would happen to the characters, laughed when they did, cringed at unnerving scenes, and I shed a few tears too.

I stopped and started on *The House on the Lake* so many times in the last two years, but even when I was having a hard time figuring out what to say, the characters stayed with me, wanting me to find the words, waking me up in the middle of the night with the echoes of their whispers still in my head. And as I pen these words at the story's completion, after the editing and revisions and tweaking, I don't know whether to jump up and down or cry. Maybe you've spent a few hours or days with these characters, but they've been in my head for years. It's going to be hard to let them go . . .and liberating too.

My characters weren't the only ones who helped me in this process. I'd like to thank my alpha readers Anne Ryan Hanafin, Scott Prussing, and Fran Tempel. You took time out of your lives to offer suggestions on how to make the story better, and I truly appreciate it! Fran, thanks for helping me with Ari's name as well. Trust me, he extends his sincere gratitude too.

I want to give a special shout-out to someone whose help has been immeasurable. Lindsey Pogue, you are *dino-mite*! Hahaha. An outstanding friend, mentor, alpha reader, cheerleader, and coach all rolled into one, I have nothing but praise for you. Thanks for being there for me.

Thanks to my fantastic beta readers too! Ann-Claire Barbier, Sarra Morgan Gray, Lauren Stabler, Kathryn Westall, and Rebecca Young, your support and words of encouragement got me to the publishing finish line. I'm grateful. It's so gratifying to talk to others about what has essentially been just in my head for so long. When I said, "Oh! What about when so-and-so did such-and-such . . ." and you understood me and responded, it was even more satisfying than when I had my first genuine conversation in French—and that's saying a lot!

To readers, thank you so much! Now, I have even more people to talk to about these characters, and they have more people who will remember them.

Finally, to my husband and my boys: I love you. I love wine too, but I don't know if I should put that in the same sentence. Oh look, I didn't! Safe! Seriously though, you three are my everything. A l'infini et au-delà pour toujours.

➤ The House on the Lake

## About the author

Holly Hill Mangin is an English literature teacher at a prestigious lycée in the south of France, a freelance copy editor at Fresh as a Daisy Editing, and the author of her first independent novel *The House on the Lake*. Always ready to laugh, Holly can be serious when the need calls for it. Currently, she's having *The House on the Lake* translated into French: *La Maison sur le Lac*. She lives with her husband and their two kids a stone's throw away from the French Riviera, and she finds that reading and writing go a long way in procrastinating learning French.

If you have a moment, please leave an honest review— without spoilers! Reviews help Indie authors like me by giving credibility to the story, allowing other readers to find it, and allowing authors to continue talking about our characters. And I'd love to continue talking about Eve, Lyn, and the rest!

Want to talk about The House on the Lake? Feel free to sign up to my Facebook author page (https://www.facebook.com/HollyMangin). I'll keep it updated with information on this story and future stories to come. Next up, the story of Eve's sister, Emma.

Printed in Great Britain
by Amazon